Grandview

Alexander Garvey Holbrook

Acknowledgements

I would like to thank the magisterial talents of Joe Stretch, Jennifer Makumbi, Lara Williams, Gregory Norminton, James Draper, Naomi Jacobs, Hanna Blakowski, Olivia Suban, John Corrigan, Jaye Kearney and Christie Calle. Without their input at the Manchester Writing School, this book would not have been possible.

Most of all, I wish to thank Nazmina Begum, who gave me the strength and the will to write against all odds.

For Naz

Manchester, 1956.

One

Her Granddad had told her about the people under the flagstones, who lay in their thousands and *gave Grandview the greenest grass.* The dark rendered them anonymous, despite the flickering light behind her. She looked around at the burning house.

The flames were an angelic white, roaring like a waterfall. Blue lights flashed in the wet tarmac. The heat lingered. She liked how it looked, but not how it felt. House fires had a smell of their own, other than smoke and flame. It was why the firemen didn't eat pork.

She had been assisting at the *scene of crime* for about a month. The children she encountered were much the same – silent, aging before her eyes. The children's homes didn't see any improvement in them. They continued, machinelike, until told to find accommodation elsewhere. They would find it in Springfield or Strangeways.

At the other end of the street, away from the fire, only one or two of the houses had lights on, but most had someone standing in the doorway. More faces appeared in the darkened upper windows. They would tell her what she already knew, or feign ignorance, or tell her to go away.

"Sheila." She looked up to the woman's voice.

"Briefing in five. Get a move on."

"Yes, Sergeant."

The woman stepped back into the darkness. Sheila paced across the flags towards the grass bank.

The burning house's eyes rolled backwards as the bricks fell inward. Voices became frantic and the firemen ran behind their engines. The roof collapsed, pushing flames into the road through the downstairs windows. The crews reappeared, all hands to the hoses, taking rhythmic steps, waiting for the fire to lash out again.

She walked across the grass and pushed herself through a gap in the railings. She rinsed her muddy shoes in a puddle at the roadside and carried on up Calter Road to her team.

They had congregated in an old bomb site. There were many gaps like it in the terraces, spaces where bodies and bricks had once been, like missing teeth. Sheila approached their huddle. Someone thrusted a large umbrella at her. She grabbed it and pushed the rusty frame, spreading the waxy, bat's wing canopy open. The men shuffled underneath and continued their conversations above her head. Dragged from wife or mistress or pint, the team stood, willing their eyes to focus or headache to subside.

A pair of saggy, squinting eyes found hers.

"Ee-arr, get us a brew, could you?"

She gave him a look, before peering over his shoulder. She raised her free hand towards the empty space at his left, moving her fingers in an arpeggio pattern.

"*Hubble bubble toil and trouble, fire burn and cauldron bubble.*"

The chatting died at her raspy spell. He looked at her, bemused.

"Sorry, Robertson, it's the brew fairy's night off."

She looked through him. Robertson smirked and looked over at the street. The conversation ambled back to life.

Can't believe these idle bleeders have mums. Or that toe rag drove bloody tanks before he started shaving.

The detectives backed off a step. She felt a nose press against her temple.

"Don't *ever* speak to a Detective like that, Kenworthy."

She turned to the gaunt face, pulled taut by an austere bun hairstyle, bent down to her eye level.

"Sorry, Sarge."

The face winced.

"Sorry, Sergeant - Sorry, Sergeant Gibbons. I'm..."

"Quiet, Constable. The Inspector's coming."

A man, whose mood they could feel from fifty paces, approached. They stopped talking. The men adopted the same stone face.

"Right, listen in, lads. They've put out the fire, near about. It were coming from the basement. They had two men inside when the roof collapsed. Didn't stand a chance."

Sheila squeezed the umbrella handle.

A runtish detective piped up from the back.

"All 'cos the bloody pakis are sacrificing their own again. Friggin' savages."

The Inspector brought down his pick-axe stare onto him.

"Boss..."

A dig in the ribs from Robertson shut him up. The Inspector's attention returned to the group.

"Point is, we wait for the all-clear, but it appears we're in the shite."

"Overtime, though."

There was a wave of shrugs and murmurs at this statement. The Inspector faced her.

"No point canvassing right now, it's too late. They'll all be talking bollocks, anyway. Go back your car and we'll let you know, girls."

Sheila and Gibbons turned about and started walking down the road towards their car. When they had covered twenty yards, Gibbons spoke to her.

"Stand fast for a second, Kenworthy."

They stopped walking.

"Have a look at them."

Sheila looked behind her at the gaggle of sniggering men in trench coats.

"Dirk Bogarde would be envious, wouldn't he?"

"Dicky Bogarde, my arse. They're a bunch of tossers, Sergeant."

"Yes, Constable. But they're dedicated tossers, nonetheless. Brave. Loyal."

Gibbons narrowed her eyes.

"*Decent.*"

She marched off. Sheila swallowed hard and followed, squeezing her gloved hands into fists at her side. They approached their Mini Cooper. The chassis rusted at the bottom and the paint had started flaking off like birch tree bark. Gibbons got into the driver's side. Sheila opened her door and looked up at the street.

The fire was now extinguished, as was all ambient sound. The firemen who had been at the face of the blaze now sat next to their engines, helmets off and panting. Beyond this, the smog settled into the street, thick from paint and plaster. The evacuated families huddled in circles, wrapped in tan blankets, saying nothing.

"Get in, Sheila, come on."

She got in and closed the door. Each inhalation was chilling and the condensation from their breath was thick. The mist ran along the bottom of the windows like welling tears. Gibbons crossed her arms and tucked her chin towards her chest. Sheila sat on her hands and rocked a little from side to side.

"Oh - do you think *that'll* work?"

"It's bloody Baltic."

Gibbons scoffed and faced forwards.

Sheila removed her right hand and dug into the footwell behind her, bringing her bag onto her lap. She flipped it open, pulled out a packet of Bourneville biscuits and shook the box at Gibbons, who looked at her with a mother's disapproval.

"Life's bad enough, Sarge."

Gibbons' expression stayed levelled on her. Sheila shook her head, took a biscuit and bit into it. Her tongue felt for wide, jagged edges on the morsels rolling around her mouth. She wanted every crunch to be air-splitting, designed to make her Sergeant sweat.

Have you ever enjoyed living, Gibbo?

The Inspector emerged from the clearing and walked towards their car. His height seemed to belong to a tree, rather than a man. He knocked on Sheila's window. She wound it down and stuck her head out, feeling the frosty air grip her face.

"We've received word from the station chief. There might be a survivor. Sorry about this, but you're going to have to hang around for a bit." He sloped away.

"Could you turn the car on please, Sergeant?"

Gibbons sighed and turned the ignition.

"If you *don't* mind..."

Sheila looked at Gibbons and removed her finger from the pattern she had been drawing on the window. What had started as a flower had become a drunken spiral as petals merged with one another. Gibbons looked away and tutted.

A group of constables and firemen without helmets emerged from the dimming haze. They were carrying stretchers to the wagons at the end of the road. Blankets covered the bodies. The firefighters had a uniformed arm or leg swinging from theirs. There was no such issue with the other bodies, as they were too small to escape the blankets. The wordless procession passed the car and out of sight.

A figure peeled away from a group of people in the distance and paced towards their car. Gibbons took Sheila by the shoulder and shook her, even though she was awake.

"Out, out!"

Gibbons threw her door open, marched around the car bonnet and stood in the road. Sheila joined her, still straightening her uniform.

"Oh, for Goodness…" Gibbons stamped over to the car, slapped the passenger door closed and stamped back.

"Stand up straight, Constable!"

Sheila drew herself up and sneered. The figure emerged, a Station Officer with a white helmet and moustache, holding a child's hand. Gibbons stepped forward and saluted.

"Sir!"

"As you were, Sergeant. Is this the Children's Officer?"

"Yes, sir. Kenworthy?"

Sheila walked over and stood before him. His black rubber leggings bulged at the thighs like aubergines. Out of his sallow complexion, his voice became sonorous and his eyes brightened.

"Now, Constable Kenworthy, this is your newest recruit, Sergeant Bibi. Can you take her to the ambulance please?"

Sheila looked down at her, saluted and smiled. The little girl was grey with ash and the dust danced in a spiral pattern around her head. Her frizzy hair looked electric in the streetlight. Her granite-like, bloodshot eyes were half open.

He reached her little hand over to Sheila and she took it.

"Come with me, love, there's a good girl."

They walked to the waiting ambulance, where the drivers were smoking. She removed her cap and looked down at the girl as she walked.

"I like your dress!"

The girl stumbled forward and said nothing.

"Bibi? That's a lovely name!"

The girl sniffled, followed by the *hub-hub-hub* of suppressed sobs. She tripped on the cobble and fell on one knee. Sheila picked her up and carried her in the crook of her arm.

"What do *you* want to be when you grow up?"

The pair reached the ambulance. The drivers flicked their cigarettes away.

"Evening gents, could you have a look at..."

Sheila heard the girl's gentle snore. The drivers stepped aside. She lay the girl down on the wooden bench in the wagon and tucked her tan blanket around her. She started walking back to the car.

"Officer?"

She stopped and turned around.

"Yes?"

The ambulance driver approached her. His eyes, pulled down at the outside and oozing empathy, focused on her sides. He took her wrists and turned her hands over. She ran to the ambulance and ripped the blanket off the girl.

The child was sleeping in a print of her own blood, which flowed from the blanket below her. Sheila turned her over, looking for the wound. A cast of blackened skin on the back of her calf stuck to the sheet and split off, revealing pink tissue. Numberless blood spots appeared and ran together like water from a sponge. One of her eyes half opened to reveal greyish whiteness. Her mouth, missing a pair of milk teeth at the front, hung open and her head lolled to the left. Sheila clenched her jaw and felt her eyes fill with stinging tears. The ambulance men pushed past her and started tending to the girl.

She careered back to the car, each shocked step landing like her knees would buckle at any second. Her shallow breath wavered, and she did not blink. She walked into the back of the Mini as the Station Officer and Gibbons talked. There were smears of blood on where she held onto its sides, trying to keep steady and control herself.

She looked up to see Gibbons' forbidding face. The Station Officer clicked his heels together and walked away. Gibbons crept towards her.

"Get a grip, Sheila."

Gibbons walked to the driver's door, got in and closed it.

Two

The Anderson Street basement had blue walls and no windows. Mould spores on the ceiling winked from behind a fresh coat of paint. The shelves - huge, drystack walls of brown evidence bags - stretched for a furlong. Sheila sat next to the door with her feet on the desk, leaning back on her chair. She had a Pasha cigarette in one hand and a magazine in the other. The Turkish tobacco masked the basement's stale aroma, leading visitors, even those who didn't smoke, to deplete her cigarette pack. She kept the top desk drawer open to fling her copy of *Future Visions* into, though no one had been down in an hour.

She still avoided bus stops, and the raised eyebrows the magazine covers attracted. As a teen, she told her mum that the ever-growing pile under her bed were her brother's, *from when he were off with a tummy bug.* These thrills still stirred her now, years later. They ran down her arms and into her jaw as her mind wandered from half-open filing cabinets or empty shelf space. She felt it rise in her as she bought her second-hand, six-shilling bundle in Levenshulme Market. It didn't matter that the vendor may as well have not been there. If she was to survive another week in Evidence, these ten copies were essential.

Two days spent underground, and she was almost done. The amateurs who wrote these tales had names like aliens. *Z.U. Neikerk, P. V. Ganani* and so on. This last story – *The Saviours of New Ganymede* – read like it had pillaged the stories that preceded it. The narrative involved little green men and big blonde ones. A battle ensued, the damage was great, the dialogue was stock. The pilot of an enormous spacecraft was scrambling around his burning hull, looking for a woman. He had the strongest chin and least memorable personality in the Solar System. His name was Brad or Blake or Blair or whatever the author deemed daring or virile in a first name.

An arm yanked him into an escape craft, hurtling him from the wreck towards a friendly planet. He turned to a porthole to *give her one last look* and his eyes widened in horror. The love interest, the McGuffin, was floating away. A nameless, underclad woman, lying in a Fay Wray supine pose across a two-page view of the great beyond. Behind her, stars pierced through the darkness like gaps in a black cross-stitch. Considering this woman was in mortal danger she looked rather relaxed. No more Captains and an infinite, pastel-smudged playground spread out all around her.

May as well go there right now. All she needs to live is a helmet and something to cover her fanny, like.

"Kenworthy."

Sheila brought down her chair's front two legs with a metallic *thwack* and flung her magazine at the drawer. It caught on the side, leaving the cover dangling over like a drunk. Gibbons paused for a second before addressing her.

"Busy?"

"No, Sergeant."

Gibbons placed a piece of paper on her desk.

"DC Cahill needs these in court tomorrow morning."
She looked back at the open drawer.

"And we'll discuss bringing stuff like that into the station after evening parade."

Gibbons walked out. Sheila slouched on her chair and took a large pull on her cigarette. She looked at the magazine cover. Another great chin in a boiler suit, shaking hands with what looked like animate lettuce. The pair of them stood in front of a city, neon-spired and with arterial tubes linking buildings.

Sheila glanced at the impassive and endless corridors of evidence. Cahill wanted the exhibits, so they were somewhere at the back. He had a knack for picking up tokens from crime scenes while his colleagues solved the cases. Sheila, over time, had relegated his 'evidence' further and further away from her desk. She exhaled, crushed her smoke underfoot, stood up, dragged the paper off the desk, and read it as she made her way to the units. As she made her way along the aisle, holes and gaps appeared as the ordering began to fall apart. *MAH726541. MAH73548. MAH73985.* The numbers meant nothing to her.

The rumour was that the basement's sodium lightbulbs were the same ones the station opened with in 1906. Only the first half of the aisle had full illumination and shadow cloaked the rest. The stench forced its way down her throat. The parcels began to show teeth and claw marks. She found the shelving ladder. Its varnish had chipped away to reveal pale, yellowing maple on each step. She reached the top and began looking at the evidence numbers in the dim light.

"2546, 5473… none of these are Cahill's. bugger it…"

She started moving the parcels out of her way with one hand. Dust particles moved like falling snow. There was a scratching sound like nails at the base of the ladder. It began scraping and getting longer, messages in a demented Morse code. She stamped her foot on the ladder and heard mice darting away into the dark. Her hands still fumbled at the back of the shelf.

"Cahill, Cahill, Cahill, Ca-hill, *Cahill*..." She half-sang each word like a chant. She carried on whisking through the parcels. Each one she turned over or pushed out the way revealed two or three more. She reached for the back of the shelf and touched the rear wall.

"Come on, DC Gormless, where're your bloody exhibits?"

Her hand carried on searching. The further her hand went, the soggier the paper got. Some hard edges poked through the paper and she nicked herself on something that felt like sharp stone. She pulled her elbow back and pushed more parcels out the way. An intact one poked through between the crumpled and mashed ones. *MAH726541*. Its creases and washed-out handwriting made it look like a prison tattoo on old skin. She grabbed the exhibit and pulled it out. Something unfurled into the vacant space.

A length of blonde hair. Long, pale strands glinting like silk in the low light. The type that she used to bury her nose in. The shade that she still found on her hairbrushes and in her sink. She bit the inside of her cheek and tensed her face as she reached for the hair and entwined it around her fingers. It was a feeling so familiar and arresting that she forgot where she was. The basement door slammed.

She jumped and looked back at her empty hands. The hair wasn't on the shelf or the ladder. She pulled evidence off the shelves, their contents clattering on the stone floor. She gritted her teeth as her search became frantic, sweeping the parcels off the shelves and rocking the ladder. The shelf was empty. She closed her eyes.

"Constable!"

Sheila grabbed Cahill's exhibit and scrambled down the ladder. She swallowed hard and yelled back.

"One mo!"

Looking towards the light next to the desk, she started kicking the parcels under the shelf. A bulky box got lodged between the shelf and the floor. Sheila carried on shifting the boxes and kicking them across the floor. She dropped to her knees and began flipping them over and pushing them away.

"At the double, Kenworthy!" Gibbons thundered.

Sheila took Cahill's parcel, stood up, shook her head and walked to her desk where Gibbons was stood. She did not break stride and came to attention behind her desk. Her breathing was beginning to settle.

"What was that, Kenworthy? That bloody racket?"

"It's, I've got Cahill's…"

"Never mind about that now."

Gibbons looked over Sheila's shoulder at the trail of parcels emerging from the aisle.

"Make yourself presentable, you're needed upstairs in ten minutes. There's been another. And call the domestics on your way up. Show some bloody initiative."

Gibbons marched out. Sheila placed the parcel on the desk, sat down and looked at it. She reached into her drawer and pulled out a small, varnished hairbrush. There was a gold and brilliant burr perched on top of stiff black bristles. She pinched one end of an errant hair in her left hand and ran it through her index and middle finger on her right like a loom. She pressed it against her nose, where it left an indentation like wire on clay.

Their Mini rocketed down Oxford Road, traffic forming a polite gap for their bells. A matinee audience spilled into the street, only for Gibbons to lean on her horn and speed up. The pedestrians jumped backwards as the Mini flew past. It wasn't until they passed St. Mary's Hospital that Sheila spoke.

"Sarge?"

Gibbons sighed.

"Sheel, there's only so much I can put up with. Pictures like that are for the inside of the men's lockers. I don't want to see you with it again, and you don't want anyone else to see you with it. Lord knows, you already bring enough attention to yourself."

Gibbons swerved left, the rear wheel clipping the kerb.

"Your locker, too, Sarge..."

The car stalled. Gibbons trained a hard gaze on Sheila.

"I beg your pardon?"

"You heard."

Gibbons sat back and half-laughed. She motioned for the cars behind her to overtake.

"You've got some bloody nerve on you, Sheel. Let's not start accusing superiors. And let's not forget who got *caught*, either."

Sheila let out an outraged chuckle and looked away. Gibbons sighed and rolled her eyes.

"No point being like that. It isn't any bloody good to anyone."

"Yes, Sergeant," Sheila coughed.

Gibbons started the car again and made the engine roar. Houses became ruins as they entered the cleared neighbourhoods. Sheila could see the smoke over the rooftops. Her stomach sank as they approached the fire.

They reached a crossroads and saw the cordon. Morris vans lay with their doors yawning open. A hive of bobbies and residents buzzed around. The police pretended to know what they were doing, and locals jostled for a view of the scene. Gibbons growled to herself and stopped the car.

"Step out of the vehicle, Constable."

Gibbons got out and closed her door. She strode to the centre of the road and straightened her back as she did for show parade. Sheila clipped her heel on the foot-well before shutting the door, knowing what came next.

"*Officers - Stand fast on your present positions!* In *close* order, gentlemen."

The police moved, wary of each step, back into a well-dressed line. Gibbons raised her head and looked from side to side.

"Ladies and gentlemen, we appreciate your concern. But please, step back and allow..."

Gibbons carried on and the residents sidled to the pavement. Sheila moved past her Sergeant and looked up towards the inner cordon. They marched through a gap made by two young police. The inner cordon did nothing to hide the scene. A heap of smoking rubble between two houses, as if some giant had taken a bite out of the terrace. Bangor ladders leant at opposite angles over the engines like marquee poles. Smoke wreathed around the whole street and the chilly air made it thicker. A group of firemen sat on the step of their vehicle. One poured the sweat out of his helmet as the other two sat in silence. Another had his back to a rear wheel, head between his knees and sobbing. The Inspector was already there, as were the detectives. They stood like men at the races, pulling on cigarettes and chatting, as the hoses were being drained around their feet and the bodies – six, burned black – were being covered.

Sheila made her way to their group. Their chatter continued around her. In front of the house, the Inspector was speaking to the Watch Officer. His white helmet was in one hand and his hair was slick with sweat. They both turned and walked over to the detectives. The Watch Officer spoke first.

"Well, get ready lads, none of you are going home tonight."

He looked at Sheila.

"Pardon me, officer, but could you get us a brew please, love? I'm gasping."

His jowls pulled down the corners of his eyes, his face an unmoving frown. Sheila almost bowed and looked about the street. She walked towards a house opposite the fire, where a woman stood was looking at her. She didn't move an inch on Sheila's thirty-yard approach.

"Excuse me, Madam..."

The woman stepped back inside and slammed her door. Sheila moved along the houses, past net curtains that fluttered like nervous eyes.

A man in a trench coat peeked from his doorway. He had a pubic carapace of hair, smeared across his pink scalp like contact marks on a billiard ball. There was a large fault line of a scar which ran across the crown of his head. An unfiltered cigarette dangled from his mouth. She paced down to him, making a point of taking her time. She stopped in front of him, noticing his lopsided and loose right cheek.

"Excuse me, sir, hate to be a mither, but do you have a kettle I could use?"

He nodded and waved the way indoors. His punch-hole eyes got smaller with his genial smile. He followed her in and kept the door open to the street. He pointed to the kitchen, saying nothing.

Sheila thought that other people's houses had an aroma about them. Most of them had notes in common. The new council houses smelled like paint pigment, like hot caulk. The houses that needed clearing stank like clogged drains, like death. This house was different. It smelt florid, despite what the man's sallow appearance suggested. There was little furniture. In the corner next to the rear window, there was a chair, a lamp and a squat bookcase with a green-rimmed Guards' cap on it. The lampshade was a deep red. There was no wireless. On the chimney breast, there was a circle pattern, with a dot in its centre, torn into the wallpaper. Spider-leg strips surrounded it. Sheila stared at it. He nudged her arm and she carried on.

His kitchen was in a similar state, wallowing in beige and magnolia. She filled up the kettle and looked over her shoulder at him. He brought out a bottle of milk and a mug. She put it on, only for him to step past her and take over, smiling at her and the kettle. Sheila turned around and again her gaze found the chimney breast. The small dot in the middle of the pattern made it look like an exploding star consuming a world. She stared at it, into it, as the jingle of a teaspoon resounded behind her. Another nudge to her arm made her turn around. He was stood, mug in hand and a lone tooth jutting like a milestone from his bottom gum.

"Did you do that, sir?"

He nodded at her, wonky smile fixed on face and grey eyes unblinking. They stood for a moment. His lips were in near constant motion, as if they searched for teeth or sections of jaw that were no longer there. She felt her nervous smile stretch like tanning leather. She took the mug, thanked him and left the house.

The Watch Officer accepted the tea and walked into the evening haze. A brief time later, the team moved to their respective duties. The Watch Officer and the Inspector shook hands and parted. The Inspector moved through the smoke and passed her the empty mug, looking as if peering over invisible pince-nez specs.

"I'm sure he'll want that back tonight, love."

She turned about, into the cloud. As she walked down the street, all sound – chatting, cascading water, cobbles clicking against her shoes – stopped. Only the streetlight bulbs were visible through the smoke. She continued to walk, trying to hear or see anything. The lights became more intense, bathing her in amber. They began to lose their hue as they banded together, becoming brilliant. She tripped on the step and the light subsided. A few detectives cackled up the street.

"No wonder we don't let you drive, you dozy cow!"

"Wankers," she muttered.

Sheila stood up, shook herself off and trudged to the man's house. She noticed he had drawn blackout curtains. She knocked on his door and waited for it to open. There was no answer. She placed the cup on his doorstep, milk drops tracing its shape onto the cardinal red step.

"Poor bloke."

Sheila jolted and turned around to the Inspector.

"Aye. Least he got the posh house, eh?"

He was deaf to her quip. They both looked through the window. The man was picking at the chimney breast wallpaper. It was hard to tell in the light, but he looked like he was dribbling a lot, his wiry spittle running down to the floor.

"Did he say anything to you? Did he see something?"

"No, sir. Smiled a lot, though."

The Inspector stepped back into the street.

"Shrapnel does that, poor bleeder. Come on, Kenworthy. You've got a survivor. It's the mum."

He started down the road at a strong pace. She followed him, but he may as well have been air. His outline was soon all that was distinguishable in the fog.

She couldn't hear her steps, only feel their thudding through her feet. The street was again masked by the smoke with only a tint of street light giving any colour. The Inspector's outline was the only thing giving her direction, and it broke in two, one heading to left and one heading straight. A needle sensation pricked Sheila's eyes and she shut them hard. She stopped in the road and squeezed the corners of her eyes. A plaster fragment glistened with eye water on her left thumb as she removed her hand. She shook her head and looked up the street, seeing the silhouette get farther and farther away. She kept walking after it.

Three

Cahill had one hand against the roof of the ambulance as he leant into it. He had his right foot crossed behind his left ankle. There was a siren-like wail coming from the cab. As she approached, Sheila could hear what he was saying.

"Calm down, love, you're alright, don't worry…"

Sheila touched him on the shoulder. He turned around and looked at her with a wry smile as the wailing continued. Sheila guided him by the shoulder away from the open doors and took him to the side.

"Cahill. How would you have liked it if someone spoke to you like that after your house got hit?"

He straightened up and the smile vanished from his face.

"Thought so. Do yourself a favour, let me do me job."

Cahill stalked away. Sheila returned to the open ambulance doors and looked in at the woman. The redness of her open, screaming mouth was the only colour about her. Ash and dust covered the rest. Some of her bottom teeth had been knocked out and one canine poked above her cut lip like a distant lighthouse. Dressings adorned her arms. She was rocking and making no sense.

"Excuse me, madam?"

The screaming began to choke itself. There were words forming. Sheila persisted.

"Madam, I'm a police officer. I need to speak to you."

The woman's mouth began to writhe as she struggled to enunciate. She looked up and drew a wheezing breath. She screamed again, louder and for longer. She was looking past Sheila's shoulder, her body shooting forward with each noise something wrenched it out of her. Sheila turned around. The residents had gathered in a huddle, marble-eyed and slack-jawed, pointing and whispering to one another. Sheila shuffled to her left to block their view. The woman was not strapped onto her gurney and had not hurled herself at anyone yet, even though her skeleton appeared to be trying to jump out her body. Sheila's hand rested on top of her baton.

"Madam, I'm here to look after you, please can we talk, madam?"

The woman's throat got hoarser, which only made her pitch become more desperate. It shifted register and timbre, an organ that someone had taken an axe to. She started slamming the back of her head into the thin pillows. Sheila stepped into the ambulance and closed the door next to her. She took off her cap and put her hand between the woman's head and the pillow. She took on a neutral tone of voice as the woman gritted her teeth.

"Please, you're only going to hurt yourself."

Sheila put her other hand on the woman's forearm. The woman's gaze snapped onto Sheila. Her tongue rolled around her mouth and Sheila made out one coughed word.

"Light."

Sheila put her head forward and the woman headbutted the side of the cab.

"It is the light!"

She fell back onto the gurney, and her breathing became quick. Her eyes rolled together and away with each blink. Each of them were reddened and had a black iris, like pebbles dropped into blood. Sheila heard the woman's phlegmy chest scratching away, turning each inhalation into a growl. Her eyes fixed on the ceiling and she breathed deep and long.

"Madam, my name is Sheila. I'm here to look after you."

The woman rolled her head to face her. Her eye colour deepened.

"My baby girls..." she half-howled. Each inhale sounded strangled by the back of her tongue. Sheila let her continue for a minute before continuing.

"I'm so sorry, love." Sheila saw her words slam into the woman like a boot.

The gurney jumped as she twitched. The wheels hit Sheila's shoe and she pulled her foot back under the bench until her heel touched the wheel arch behind her.

"It is the light, it is the light." the woman wheezed. Her face began to look contented beneath the plaster dust, now collecting into small rolls on her forehead and cheeks. Sheila stirred in her seat.

"Madam, can you think of anyone who would want to hurt you?"

The woman opened her mouth, only to clench her jaw again. Her top teeth pushed the solitary canine out of the jaw like a drawbridge.

"Did your husband..."

The woman's expression cracked like glass as she sprang up, pressing her nose against Sheila's.

"Mind your own fucking business!" She shrieked. Sheila did not stir. The woman slammed her body backwards before she swung her arm loose. She faced the ceiling and a smile rolled across her face. Sheila made her right hand into a fist.

"Madam?"

The woman began whispering and repeating herself.

"It is the light. It is the light. It is the light." She raised both of her hands and rested them on her lap. The fingers on her left scratched at the dressing on her right forearm. Some of her fingernails were missing, others broken in half as though erased.

Sheila opened the door and left her. The Inspector was stood next to the bodies and talking to Cahill. She stood next to him and sighed.

"Sir, I think that..."

"It was her?" Cahill looked at Sheila with raised eyebrows.

"Well, no Cahill, I didn't think..."

"Because you already know that she was downstairs while the rest of the family cooked, right?" Cahill's eyes widened, searching for a victory, any victory, over her. The Inspector clocked Cahill on the back of the head, knocking the expression off his face.

"Shut it, grasshopper."

"Aye, boss." Cahill loped off.

"What did you find out, Constable?" The Inspector looked around after asking the question, as if the answer would fall out of the air.

"Her brain's knackered, sir. She's one for Springfield."

"Get anything from her?

"Not really. She kept saying something about it *being the light* or something."

"You what?"

"She said 'it is the light, it is the light' over and over again."

"And?"

Sheila wrinkled her top lip and looked away.

"Reckon he battered her?" he asked.

"Probably, sir. She told me to mind me own fucking business."

The Inspector shrugged.

"Shame. Find your Sergeant, Kenworthy. We've got a neighbourhood to canvas."

They carried on down the street, away from the main scene. Sheila could see Gibbons working through the houses on the opposite side of the road. As the Sergeant made her way along the houses, the lights would turn off. She would knock twice and then move on to the next house. When she was two or three doors down, the previous houses would come to life again.

Sheila sauntered across the road to where the lights had come back on. She rapped on the door with a stern and sharp knock.

"Police! Open the door!" The men reserved such a tone for a raid. She looked to her left at Gibbons, whose attention had been seized mid-knock. Sheila knocked again, this time heavier and slower. The door flew open. A young woman with steely eyes and pinched features leant into Sheila's face.

"Fuck do you want, Copper? I've got two little 'uns here and an 'usband on nights."

"Erm..."

Sheila flinched as the door banged shut. She turned to her left and caught up to Gibbons, still knocking on houses that were playing dead. There was nothing said as they trudged along, getting the same mute response from every door. They crossed the road and continued along the opposite houses, which may as well have had stone doors. All was shrugs and hums as the men stood in a schoolboy huddle, opening fag packets and reaching for flasks. The Inspector arrived and approached the officers. They both stood to attention as he stood before them.

"Right, girls, that's enough for one day. See you at refs and parade, alright?"

He walked away. Sheila looked at Gibbons' narrowed eyes.

"*Police, open the door?* Really? Come on, Sheel," Gibbons sneered.

Rodney, the neighbour's cat, was the brightest coloured cat in Manchester. He had a knack of being outside when the dye factory clouds would settle on the neighbourhood. Today his white fur was bishop's purple. It didn't stop him licking his paw as Sheila walked up to the gate. She rubbed his head and he purred in a manner closer to a croak before squeezing through her hands and continuing his patrol across the garden walls. She opened the gate, the swollen wood pushing through the grey paint.

She reached through the letterbox and pulled a length of string from the other side which had her key attached. Sheila opened the door and stepped inside. Her eyes met those of a rakish, aproned woman in the hallway.

"Evening, Alice," she said. Sheila closed the door and walked past her, towards the kitchen.

"Have they caught anyone yet?" Alice asked in a rattling voice. Sheila tore a scrap of bread from the loaf on the worktop.

"Don't think there's anyone to catch. People going soft in the head in old houses."

"Bloody council. Pay peanuts, get monkeys, bloody scoundrels..." Alice muttered. Her apron used to be a butcher's and hid her feet which, with her tiny steps, always gave her the illusion of being on her tip toes. Sheila tore another clump of bread from the loaf and leant in the doorway while Alice sat down in a simple chair with a simple cushion next to her wireless set. There was a telegram, crooked and yellowing like an old tooth, on the radio unit.

"Any news from the Ministry?" Sheila asked.

"Missing, still. He'll be surrounded by a bunch of chink tarts in some hole, no doubt."

"You don't know that, love, wait for news, like."

"Yes, yes. By the way, these came for you today, Sheel." Alice reached behind her chair and lifted a thick package out. It bore an airmail stamp and a return address to New Jersey.

"Ah, fantastic, cheers!" Sheila took the dense envelope and hugged it. Alice scratched her scalp past grey hairs.

"You're ten in your head, you. Ten-year-old boy, at that!"

Sheila dropped her arms to her side, letting the package bump against her hip.

"Jesus, Al, I said thanks, didn't I?"

"Sorry, you did, you're welcome. Any *visitors* tonight?"

"Not tonight. Going Imperial for the double bill."

"God, really? Smelling like feet and old cigs?"

"My absolute favourite" Sheila said, and smacked her lips.

"Shurrup, sheel. I'll never get the appeal of paying to get bloody terrified, you know. Right, bugger off now, listening to me programme."

Sheila turned around.

"Oh, Sheel, love, hang on..." Alice reached behind the radio and pulled out three letters. Sheila's heart sank as she recognised her handwriting on the envelopes.

"Thanks, Alice" she murmured, and took them.

Alice turned the switch on the wireless and angled her body towards to speaker, almost as if she had turned herself off. Sheila turned around and made her way up the stairs to her room.

The bed had grey sheets on an old mattress and thin pillows. Her wardrobe had one door open, around which her clothes sprawled off their hangers like vines through an old window. She cast the letters and package onto the bed. She took her tunic off, lay on the bed and picked up the letters.

A stroke of red lacerated across her handwriting. The same colour pen declared, in angular letters, NOT KNOWN AT THIS ADDRESS.

Sheila lifted the dry flap, crisp from old adhesive, and pulled out the letter.

17th January, 1956.

Dear Marion,

Sheila scrambled the letter back in its envelope. She grabbed a fresh blue blouse from the pile of clothes on the windowsill. There were three shillings next to the clothes, which she took in her hand before grabbing a cardigan, which hung from the wardrobe door, picking up a tobacco tin and leaving the room. The cacophony of *The Goon Show* roared out of the front room, but Alice never laughed. Sheila caught a glimpse of her as she made her way out of the house - bolt upright, unblinking and no light behind the eyes.

There was no one at the stop and it was cold. She stood there and looked on as the streetlights flickered into life as the grey dusk began to darken. The shadows cast by the avenue trees grew darker and the lights brightened at the end of the road, as if Sheila was in the cornea of an immense closing eye. A rattling engine announced itself and the beige, mud-speckled bus ambled up to Sheila's stop.

A few minutes later and she was stood on the pavement outside the *Imperial* cinema. The red and black lettering stood like music on staves and proclaimed a *midnite* double bill of *X: The Unknown* and *The Quatermass Xperiment*. Both had X certificates and that meant no one in this Thursday night. The boy in the booth rested his head on the glass and his chin on the countertop, resigned to making his own fun. He looked at Sheila and his eyes met hers, before he ticked his head to the left and carried on staring ahead. Sheila walked past him and beamed. She walked through the swing doors, into the murky space.

The dim wall lights were muted further by the maroon carpets and walls. There was a couple sat closer to the screen on the left. They appeared relaxed, but were not leaning on one another. Sheila took her seat – centre block, rear row, right-hand aisle seat – and took out her tobacco tin. It did not shine and had a portrait of a young man, but only from the chin downwards. Everything up from there had been rubbed off over time. She opened it and took out a pre-rolled cigarette, shaking the excess tobacco back into the tin where it stuck on the little pile already there. The book of matches only had five left. She stuck her match on the back of the seat in front of her and lit up. Her eyes wandered back to the couple. The screen was still blank and yet they were staring at the screen anyway, as though they were in a gallery.

The projectionist rattled around his booth, the clicking and stamping of metal sounding like the mechanism of a great opening door. The lights went out and the screen lit up. Sheila watched the couple shrink closer together as the tritone violins shrieked over opening credits, melting away to reveal the jagged X of the title.

Over the next ninety minutes, she ignored the film and watched the couple. She saw them jump and swear in unison, before settling deeper into each other's arms each time. By the end, the woman had her head buried in the man's neck and he had his hands clasped around her. From what Sheila could see, he also had his eyes closed during the more scary sequences, too. Sheila knew the glowing 'monster' was literal fried tripe and chuckled to herself. She picked up her tobacco tin, took out another roll-up and lit it with her final match. Her gaze found the seat next to her.

She reached out and put her hand on it, leaning into her weight and closing her eyes, clamping her cigarette between her teeth. She longed for the head of blonde hair she had rested hers on. They had sat like this for hours like piles of balanced rocks. They had waited until the audience had filed out and then kissed like wolves in the darkness.

A bombastic fanfare blarted over the end title and the lights came up. Sheila saw that she had dug her nails into the fabric of the next chair along and withdrew her hand. She grabbed her cardigan and her tobacco tin before making her way into the lobby. The kiosk was closing, so she took a book of matches and left a sixpence on the counter top before heading outside. Her quick steps did not abate until she was around the corner, past her bus stop and into the streets next to Alexandra Park.

Orange streetlight came through her cotton curtains like radiation. She lay on the bed and had the envelope next to her. One corner poked through the flap. She thumbed it open and pulled the letter out. Her index finger flipped it open and she took a deep breath.

Sorry I've not written to you for a bit. I've been up to my eyes in all this bloody business in Grandview. I really wish I had someone to talk to here. The days are long, and I might have to throttle Cooper in the near future.

I'm sick of Anderson Street now. Our lord and saviour Gibbo wants me gone. Old bag doesn't appear when Fletch puts on lippy or when DCI Wolfe takes a cadet to the back of his car but does when I'm smoking a rollie instead of a straight. Keep expecting her to whip her belt out and have me across her lap, the cow.

I keep finding stuff of yours here. Sick of telling you that you need your sodding hair cutting, you know. Always find a bit on me dresses or one in the sink, still. You left a little hairbrush here. Thought a mouse had got in my bedside drawer and I damn nearly screamed.

How are you getting on, love? Gibbo told me that you'd recovered and were going to Lancs Constab. I couldn't believe you'd be fit for owt. Last time I saw anyone in one of them frigging machines was when our Robert was dying. Bloody Gibbo told me about your transfer. Could have killed her for that.

Alice keeps asking when you'll be back. I haven't told her because she'd be a pain in the arse crying. I'll tell her one day.

Please write back.

Love you,

Sheel.

She dropped the letter onto her chest let her arm fall onto the bed.

Four

"There's a group of people, worship the devil and that, and I think one of them's a City fan, no, no, think there's a bunch of City fans, who are roasting babies on spits and..."

Sheila held the phone between her shoulder and ear, pencilling *nutter* into her time log and picking up her brew. Her undisguised slurp of contempt down the receiver did not stop the raving on the other end.

"...and I'll tell you everything, yeah, I'll tell you everything, but I want paying first. Like a reward and that?"

Sheila paused and let the correspondent breathe into the receiver.

"Well sir, please may I take your name down?"

"Yes, my fine constable, it's Joseph Goebbels von Cock-Mouth..."

Sheila swatted the phone hook down like a cockroach. The room had so many phones ringing that only hammering was distinct, the inner workings of a huge sonorous drill. Across from Sheila sat Fletcher. Her nasal, Collyhurst drawl managed to cut through it all like a gate turning on rusty hinges.

"Darling, could you describe to me what you know? Right, let me just get this down..." Her eyes didn't look around so much as float above or sink below everyone else's gaze. She picked up a pencil and scratched the edge of her nose with the eraser end. Sheila tore a scrap off the top of her time log and scribbled *day release?* before rolling it up and throwing it across the table. Fletcher dropped her pencil and picked up the paper, unfurled it and nodded.

"Thank you sir, I'll be sure to remind Her Majesty to tell the Prime Minister his bedtime story, goodbye." Fletcher hung up and shook her head. Sheila crossed her eyes and let her mouth hang open.

"Have you been refs yet, Fletch?"

"Nope. Belly's roaring, like."

"Aye, and what a bloody belly, too."

"Bugger off, Sheel. You had yours?"

"No. Think its corned beef butties again."

"Fuck me, do this lot still think they're in bloody Burma?"

They went quiet again as Fletcher's phone rang. She let it ring and hoped it would stop.

"May as well be, Fletch. Least they could shoot back." Sheila nodded up at the phone and Fletcher sighed, before picking it up. This was part of the routine of whenever there was a public appeal. Gibbons would take a leave of absence, Sheila would be brought from the basement to man the phones and the days would melt together as the mad and the maddening emerged on the line.

Sheila's phone log had the word *nutter* all over it and had become more manic the more it had to be written, the letters becoming larger and their spacing becoming more erratic. Doodles sprouted from the serifs of her handwriting and onto the margins, great creepers which trailed the length of the page and split off into faces or shapes or spirals at some points. The Inspector arrived as Sheila put her pencil down. He leant over her shoulder and scanned over her work.

"Not a bad effort, there, Sheel. That's another logbook that we can't get back."

"Do you want to swap, sir?" Sheila looked up at his dour face.

"Not especially, love. Just look like you give a toss, eh?" He took the phone log and closed it.

"I'll do me best." He walked away.

Exasperated faces drooped and sagged at every telephone. The Inspector sat and chain smoked. Cadets were moving boxes of paper from room to room in a constant procession. They had moved so much over the week that they looked choreographed, moving in squares or figures of eight to avoid stepping on each other's feet. No papers fell anymore. A pair of plainclothesmen sat in the corner office waiting for their orders and began cackling, ambushing people's attention.

Sheila looked up at the clock.

"Sir?"

"What do you want, Kenworthy?" He shouted.

"When're relief getting here?"

"An hour and a half ago, but Wolfe's got them canvassing. Suck it up."

He returned to his paper and lit another cigarette.

Sheila's phone rang and she answered.

"City of Manchester Police," she said. There was silence on the other end of the line.

"Hello?"

The silence continued before the phone hung up. Fletcher, who had been repeating varieties of *umms* and *aahs*, hung up a second later.

"Anything new, Sheel?"

"Well, the not-rights are out in force."

"Aye, I know. Going refs, cover me phone, darling."

"Eh up, cheeky bint…"

Fletcher stood up and strolled over to the exit. Sheila yelled out.

"Ee-arr, boss?"

"She can go."

"Why, though!"

"Because I sodding well say so, Sheel, you said they're only nutters, didn't you?"

"Yeah boss, I did." Sheila's tone fell on itself and she found herself meeting the Inspector's look of annoyance. He in turn looked over at Fletcher, who blew a kiss at him before filing out.

"So, get on the phones, misery guts." He turned the page of his paper and drew it over his face. Sheila dragged her chair around, making the legs screech and moan against the floor. She had the eyes of everyone in the room.

"Balls to this." The Inspector stood up and took his paper into the corner office, his finger marking the page with the 2:30 Belle Vue odds. The two plainclothesmen stumbled out a second later. The door slammed shut and the wireless clicked on, filling the little office with crowd noise.

Fletcher's phone rang. Sheila picked up a pencil and stooped over Fletcher's logbook. She answered the phone.

"City of Manchester Police."

The breathing on the other end became fevered. Sheila adopted a schoolmarm's tone in her reply.

"Pardon me, sir, for it can only be a sir, but do you think you're being in *any way* clever by acting like this when we're looking for..."

"It is the light." The phone line cut. Sheila froze. She wrote down the words in Fletcher's log, put the receiver down and walked to the corner office. Her knocks lost all restraint, from solid raps to open-handed bangs. The Inspector stamped around the desk and pulled the door open.

"Are you trying to make me hit you or something, Sheel?"

"Sir, I've just had a phone call, made me think..."

"Thinking's not your remit, love, make a note of it and go away. I'm looking at ante post odds on the dogs."

He shut the door. The room had become quieter beneath the ringing phones. Fletcher stood in the doorway, half-eaten sandwich in hand.

"Fuck me dead, it's Miss Marple!" she exclaimed through crumby lips.

The room laughed and Sheila rolled her eyes. She walked back to her station where both terminals chimed at once, pencils and mugs jangling along in discordant harmony. She sat and watched them ring out.

They walked in step towards Booth Hall hospital as soft rain fell on the empty streets and beat against their caps. The outpatients' entrance had concerned, sleep-deprived parents hovering around it. Sheila and Fletcher excused themselves and walked into the lobby. The hubbub of children – wailing, laughing, clapping, chatting – bounced off the walls as adults sat, totem-like, amidst the sea of little ones. The two officers approached the nurse behind the desk. Her short red hair burst from her linen cap, which rested on the back of her head, and she beamed at them.

"Excuse me, can you point us towards the burns ward?" Sheila asked. The nurse's beam faded and she got up, nodding and motioning for them to come around into the corridor.

"Drama queen," Fletcher mumbled.

"Like you'd want to stay in here, Fletch, you'd end up frigging flinging them," Sheila clipped back. They made their way through the double doors and the nurse motioned for them to follow her into a curtained cubicle. She looked up at them.

"Erm, just so you know, it's not good."

"You what?"

"You're here to see Bibi, right?"

"Yes, we are." Sheila's stomach dropped and her heart slowed.

"I'm sorry, but she collapsed a couple of days ago. She's been non-responsive since. We're not hopeful."

They stood in silence.

"Can we see her?" Fletcher's voice remained unmoved.

The nurse nodded and walked past them both. They followed her down the long, cold corridors and the sound of people gave way to the sounds of machines and apparatuses, keeping hearts beating and lungs inflating. Dusk tinted the rain clouds lilac through the tall windows. They turned down one long straight corridor next to a quadrangle. Everything went still and quiet. Their steps lost their echo on the thin carpet. Five rooms, all doors closed and the lights off in all but the centre one. The nurse peeked through the small window in the door and pushed the door open, holding it open for the officers. Sheila turned and stopped at the door. Fletcher bumped into her back, nudging her into the room. The nurse stepped to her right and Fletcher stepped to her left. The door clicked closed.

The ventilator shook and squeaked, forcing air into the small body on the small bed. Her eyes were half open, the pupils at opposite corners like loose buttons, much as they had been when Sheila had last seen her. An eerie quiet fell on them as they looked at her. Sheila glanced at the walls. There were drawings. Outstretched and wide-palmed arms on square bodies, misshapen smiling faces, cigar-shaped cats and dogs with rope-like tails beneath a lemon sun.

The sun looked peculiar. Unlike everything else, it looked proportionate and even had slight shading. Skinny strips of yellow stretched from a neat, round centre. It was the same in all the drawings.

"Did she draw all of these herself?" Sheila inquired, pointing at the walls.

"I'm sorry, I don't know," the nurse returned.

"Well, she wouldn't have had many visitors, that's for sure," Fletcher interjected. Sheila shot her a look and knocked her heel with her foot. The room fell back in quiet.

"Has she had anyone come and see her?"

"A couple of people just after she was admitted, but no one since. We put those up, officer. Wanted to make her as comfy as possible in case she went."

Sheila walked around the bed to one of the pictures. There was one figure in a dress under the sun.

"Do you mind if I take this back with me?"

"Bloody ell, Sheel, you feeling alright?" Fletcher looked at her with wide eyes under ridged brows and an open mouth. The nurse had a similar look, tinged with outrage.

"May I?"

The nurse paused and said, "Is that really necessary?"

"Yes. Police business." Sheila held her tone as they held their gaze.

"Yeah. But bring it back, soon as."

Sheila took the drawing pin out of the top of the drawing and took it off the wall. She folded it as she approached the nurse, who opened the door and didn't break her steely look. Fletcher shook her head in amazement and followed Sheila out.

Their exit was much quicker than their entrance as the nurse pounded down the corridors, sidling behind her desk and ignoring the officers as they left the building. They made half a mile towards Rochdale Road before Fletcher spoke.

"Sheila, do you need a day off or summat?"

"No Fletch, I think there's something here."

"I don't wanna know. Wolfe'll drop a bollock if you show him."

"Don't care, its important."

"Ey, Miss fucking Marple, they'll bloody laugh you out of the office. Give it back."

"What's your fucking issue, Fletch?"

"That you're going doolally on me, Sheel. I like you, you know, but your fucking bonkers and you're trying to be all sleuthy. People are horrible to one another, part of the job, get over it. Now, give the sodding picture back."

They were still for a moment. The streetlight darkened Fletcher's make up, giving her black lips and hollow eyes under her cap in the amber glow. Sheila grimaced and continued to walk up the road. Fletcher caught up to her and they continued walking to Rochdale Road, to catch a bus back to Anderson Street station. They did not speak and let their gazes wander up the street. People would catch their eye and either look away at the floor or hold their stares for a few seconds. This continued for five minutes before a Piccadilly bus pulled up. They got on and sat down. Smog was settling over the skyline and the streets were empty.

"They'll have your head on a plate," Fletcher said.

They arrived a brief time later. The rain had picked up, running down in streams to Peter Street. Sheila marched into the station and picked up her pace towards the great wooden staircase in the lobby. Her feet felt light, booming on each quick step up the stairs towards the incident room. She opened the wooden door and did not close it behind her. A skeleton staff remained on the phones, which no longer rang. The Inspector was still sat in the corner office, logbooks on his desk and ashtray overflowing. He looked up and caught her gaze as she entered the room and closed the door behind her.

"What bloody time do you call this, Kenworthy?"

"Sorry, sir, but there's something I need to tell to you..."

"Sit down, constable."

Sheila took a seat opposite him and his eyes narrowed.

"Go on, Sheel. I'm all ears." His tone had deepened.

Sheila took the paper out of her bag and unfolded it. The ink had run on little spots. She placed the picture on his desk.

"Sir, look at that pattern."

He looked, closed his eyes and tilted his head back, mouth open and struggling to hold on to his words.

"Are - are you taking the piss, Sheel?" He exclaimed. Sheila felt stunned for a second before gathering herself and leaning forward.

"I saw that *exact* same pattern in that bloke's house in Grandview."

"What bloke?"

"The bloke with the buggered face, the one who were dribbling."

The Inspector sighed in irritation and squeezed his jaw closed.

"Sheel. He had half his brain missing. And where did you get this drawing?"

His face turned from vexed irritation to plain anger in half a second.

"Christ, Sheila..."

"I saw it in Booth Hall, sir..."

The Inspector banged the table with his fist and put his hand to his forehead.

"For the love of God, Sheila. What's wrong with you?"

"Sir, please, let me explain." She felt her voice begin to shake. He let his hand fall from his face onto the desk, with a dull thud.

"You have thirty seconds, constable."

"I saw that pattern on the man's chimney breast and on Bibi's drawings. They lived a street from each other. He could be a not-right, but I'm not sure. Also, look at my logbook. Someone said *it is the light* to me and hung up, that's what the woman we dealt with said."

The Inspector looked at her for a moment.

"Meaning what?"

"That could be our tit-for-tat there, sir, could be a conspiracy. I know there's not a lot, but it's something!"

He sat up in his chair.

"So, you have deduced that this is a tit-for-tat thing, a thing we worked out a month ago, from the testimony of a pair of nutters, a drawing done by a nutter and a drawing done by an orphan girl? And, on top of everything, you bloody well took it while she's bloody well suffering? Alone! Have I got this right?"

Sheila started to panic.

"We need leads, sir, this is a lead, it's evidence..."

"No it's not, constable. It's drivel. It is not your job to gather evidence. Get a lift and give it back. Dismissed."

He opened a logbook on a random page and ran his finger down the names. Sheila stood up and took the drawing from the desk, folded it back up and put it into her bag.

She was quiet on the car journey. An officer from traffic who she ran into in the lobby gave her a swift ride to the hospital and came to an abrupt stop outside the outpatients' entrance. Sheila got out and ran up the steps towards the lobby. The same nurse saw her as she entered and stood up to meet her.

"Officer?"

"I've brought the bloody picture back..."

"Officer, can you come in here please?" She spoke the words like a statement, swallowing her tone.

"I'm giving it back, for goodness sake...."

A woman stepped out of a curtain cubicle in front of her, wearing a navy uniform and a veil embossed with a red cross, as if she had stepped out of the hospital walls themselves.

"Err, excuse me!" The woman growled. Sheila stopped. The nurse called over to the woman.

"I'm sorry, Sister, she wouldn't stop."

"That's alright, go back behind the desk" the Sister said back, keeping her eye on Sheila. The nurse left and closed the door behind her.

"Step this way please, officer."

The Sister led Sheila into the cubicle and drew it closed. She turned to face Sheila and spoke with a low and commanding voice.

"Firstly, don't be difficult on my ward, I don't care who you are. Second of all, you're late."

"Sorry?"

"Bibi. We didn't resuscitate."

Sheila looked around for a chair. She ended up looking back at the Sister.

"Was there anyone with her?"

"An aunt. She's down there now, if you need to talk to her."

"I would, please."

The Sister strolled past Sheila and down those same corridors, towards the same room now imbued with a tomblike silence. The Sister stopped at the top of the corridor and stood at ease, watching Sheila make her way down to the room. There was a woman stood at the huge corridor window, her head hanging low beneath a black hijab, eyes closed and mumbling. Sheila placed her steps, swapping her heel's boom for her toe's tap. She stood at the entrance to the room and listened to the woman.

"Bismallah ihrahmani Raheem..."

The room was empty now, save for two porters who were wiping down the bare bed. The pictures had disappeared from the walls and only their pin holes remained. Sheila felt them stare at her like a jury. In her hand, the paper felt like an impossible weight and she let it flutter to the floor.

"Is that one of Bibi's?" The voice was fractured. Sheila turned her head as if it might fall off at any second. The woman in the hijab stood and wrung her hands. Her eyes were inflamed by both tears and rage.

"Yes, it is, I'm really sorry, I had no idea..." Sheila began and then faltered. The woman pushed her out of the way and snatched the paper up from the floor. She stood as straight as a lance and looked at Sheila, nose to nose and with trembling lips.

"You don't know about much, do you, *toi hendikath*?" She pressed the paper against Sheila's collarbone, knocking her back a step, before walking away with her hand to her eyes. The Sister appeared and stood, waiting. Sheila took the paper, now creased and with a small tear from the woman's fingernail and placed it into her bag.

"If you don't mind, officer, we have to prepare for another patient," The Sister stated, looking into the middle distance as though at attention. Sheila stepped out of the room and headed down the corridor. The light was dull as she made her way back to the stone corridors. The bulbs in the wards began to flutter into life like a hundred opening eyes. All around the quadrangle the corridor lights began twitching. The ones on her corridor reflected off the windows and placed them in the lilac sky. She turned onto the corridor and walked down towards the front desk. She stepped onto the street and the rain began to slalom in great waves across the pavement and the traffic car, its engine still running. She opened the door and got in. He looked over at her and smiled.

"You manage to give it back? You alright?"

Sheila had clenched her jaw, swallowing sobs back in a final effort to not weep.

"Yeah, I'm fine," she half-mouthed.

"Alright, then." He set off towards Anderson Street. As they reached the corner of Rochdale Road, Sheila saw a figure, kneeling on the corner in the rain. The driver wound down his window. It was a woman. Her hijab gripped her head in the storm.

"Are you alright there, madam?" the driver shouted through the rain. Her head rose and she met Sheila's eyes. She staggered to her feet, the smog parting with each step as though giving her room. Her features became wilder and wilder with each step she took until she reached the car, swinging at the door and chassis with her arms, screaming the whole time. She aimed open palms and hammer fists at the driver, who raised his arm off the wheel.

"Bloody hell, can you help me here, love?" he cried out as the flurry of blows did not relent. He fumbled for the car door handle with his free hand. Sheila unbuckled herself and ran around the front of the car as the driver flung his door open, knocking the woman backwards. Sheila fell on her, clasping her arms around the woman's arms as she kicked and rolled and bawled.

Sheila held onto her tight, feeling her thrashing subside into rocking. The woman buried her head into Sheila's neck and sobbed. The driver stood over them both and prepared a pair of handcuffs.

"Fucking hell fire, look at her!"

"Not interested, love, count her lucky I didn't belt her in't mouth." He stooped down and fastened a cuff onto the woman's wrist and pulled her up by her underarm. She cried in a tone of defeat as they led her to the car.

Sheila walked through the pooling rain to the car and pulled the rear passenger door open. The woman moaned as he put her into the car. He closed her door and got in. The woman put her head against the window, where the moisture on head and the window steam cut a spectral figure. Sheila walked round the bonnet and got into her seat.

"I'll deal with her when we get to the nick," Sheila said. He half-laughed and motioned with his head to the woman.

"Bloody see that you do..."

Five

"Got one for the tank here, Sarge, she had a go at me and Jack!"

The Desk Sergeant glanced over his ledger and nodded her through. The woman was still murmuring and staggered down the corridor to the cells. An inmate yelped and wailed behind her iron door, a portal to a nightmare.

"Where are you taking me?" the woman managed.

"Out of the rain and away from my colleague. He wasn't lying about giving you a slap," Sheila replied. The corridor got quieter as they reached the end. There was a cell open, the bed a mattress with no blanket. Sheila sat the woman down. She was still crying and shivering.

"I need to talk to you as well. You look like you'll catch your death. Would you like a cup of tea?"

The woman nodded and wrapped her arms around herself.

The woman hunched under the blanket, both her hands trembling around the tea. Her fingers must have been burning on the tin mug, but she did not move them. The steam from the tea met her soaking face, making droplets on her nose which ran onto her top lip. Sheila sat and watched her, her seat backed against the sidewall so she could see into the corridor.

"You feeling a bit warmer?"

The woman nodded, although her head still hung.

"Do you need anything else?"

The woman shook her head.

"What's your name?"

"Safa...Hussein."

"I'm really sorry for your loss, Safa."

Safa looked up.

"I don't know what to do. I have nothing left."

She closed her eyes and her chin sank back into her chest. She swayed to her left and rock backwards up the bed, so that her feet dangled a couple of inches off the floor.

"Could there be anyone you know about who'd want to hurt you?"

There was a long pause.

"You can't protect us."

"Excuse me?"

"This city is full of people who want people like me dead. Including here. You're only helping them."

Sheila leant forward onto her knees and sighed.

"If it weren't for me, you'd be in here for assaulting a copper. You're right, we've got a fair few crap coppers, but they're not evil."

Safa took a gulp of her drink and put it on the floor between her feet.

"You're just as stupid as I thought."

Sheila got to her feet and picked up her bag.

"I'll let you be by yourself for a bit. Enjoy your tea and I'll see you in the morning." She stepped into the corridor and began to make her way out. A lightning flash pulsed through the high windows and across the ceiling and the lightbulbs twinkled for an instant.

"It is the light!"

Sheila's shoe squeaked as she came to a stop.

"That's what they say, isn't it?" Safa called out behind her. Sheila turned to see Safa, unsteady on her feet, in the doorway of her cell. Her clothing still clung to her in places, as if she had parts of her torso missing. Sheila made her way back down to her.

"Who?"

"Them," Safa said, rolling her eyes up at the ceiling and making her way back into the cell. She climbed onto her bed, with her back to Sheila.

Sheila approached the bed and prodded her in the back. Safa turned over, her face a mask of hatred. Sheila opened her bag and produced the picture, unfolding it and stretching it out.

"What can you tell me about this picture?"

Safa swallowed and her eyes softened.

"It's Bibi's."

"That sun – did she draw that?"

Safa's mouth tightened and her eyes squeezed closed.

"Yes. After she met them."

"Who are they, madam?"

Safa rolled onto her back.

"I couldn't believe how well they treated us when we first arrived."

Sheila sat on the end of the bed, which gave out a throaty creak. Safa watched Sheila for a second.

"They?"

"Oh, come on now. There are families we know – knew – who never spoke to their neighbours. Ours always smiled at us, talked to us. We thought it was paradise…"

Sheila gave her a pitying look. Safa carried on.

"There was a man. He didn't live on the street. His face was cut up. He never talked. He just stared."

Sheila gripped the mattress with one hand out of Safa's sight.

"Who is he, madam?"

"I don't know. I asked the people on the road who he was, and they said nothing. They would stand there, smiling or looking at me, but never say anything. It was like I wasn't speaking in English. And he came back, every day."

"What happened, madam?"

"My brother invited him in. He came around many times. I don't know his name or what they talked about, but my brother was obsessed. He kept repeating himself, *it is the light, it is the light.* He kept drawing that symbol on things, backs of envelopes, old newspaper, anything paper. Bibi started doing it as well. She loved him."

Safa trailed off and rolled over.

"Madam, have you seen this man since the fire?"

"No, I have not."

"Do you have any idea where he lived?"

"Somewhere close. Go back to Grandview. Ask them. I'm tired now, leave me alone."

A moment later, Safa was snoring. Sheila closed her cell door and pounded up the corridor. She skipped up the steps towards the front desk. The Desk Sergeant caught her eye.

"Who was that?"

"She's a drunk, sarge, couldn't get any sense out of her. Given her a brew and a blanket and she'll be right. I'll let you know when I know more."

The Desk Sergeant grunted and continued with his crossword. Sheila continued through the emptying station. The offices were all dark now, except for one, which remained open all hours on the top floor. Filing cabinets and yellowing paper filled these offices, rather than desks. The surfaces of the windowsills had thin layers of dust and the dried bodies of insects lay like rocks poking through snow. Sheila saw the wooden staircase to the department.

The stairs were missing their carpet. Old nails stuck out of the cheap wood. As she neared the top, the air became thick with cigarette smoke and the voices got louder and boorish. The only light came from a single glass panel in the door at the top of the stairs. She looked at the peeling vinyl letters and the ghosts of old ones.

City of Manchester Police

Criminal Investigation Department

The door shuddered open and she walked inside. She felt the office temperature cool as she made her way across the room. Conversations turned furtive. Looks became glances. Mouths held back smirks. She gripped the inside of her lower lip between her front teeth.

She reached the kitchen station across the office and the pot was still hot. It already had milk in it. She poured and picked up the brew, small spots of scum bobbing around it. She heard a man exhale to her right. He pulled on a cigarette and leaned against the countertop. He regarded her like a cat stalking a bird. His hooded eyes rested on her and he exhaled his smoke out of the corner of his mouth. She smiled, flicked the Vs at him and headed towards the corner office. A pronounced, nasal *meow* followed her, as did a series of deep chuckles. She knocked on the corner office door.

"Enter."

Detective Chief Inspector Wolfe sat behind his desk. Mustard folders, old statements and outstanding warrants lay scattered across it. He did not look up as she entered his office and closed the door behind her, nor when she placed the mug on his desk.

"Cheers for that."

He took a sip of his tea and pursed his lips. He still did not look up. Sheila announced herself.

"Sir, do you have a minute?"

"Yes, sit down," he said.

She took a seat. He hung his hollow gaze on her like a noose. She bored into his eyes before drawing a slow blink.

"Having an alright day, Sheel?"

"Sir?"

"It *is* Sheila right, Sheila Kenworthy?"

"Yes, sir. I hope you don't mind me coming in this late."

"It's alright, we're winding down for the night. My second-in-command speaks highly of you, you know."

"Thank you, sir."

He stayed stationary for a moment before he spoke again.

"Well, what can I do for you, constable?" he probed. She sat up in her seat and shook her head a little.

"Yes, of course, sir. Sir, I think there's something dodgy going on in Grandview."

"As always."

"This is different, sir. I think the people who are doing the arsons know each other, sir."

The office was silent. He looked at her, confused.

"How can that be?"

She produced the picture from her bag and put it on his desk.

"This picture, sir. It belonged to Bibi Hussein. Look at that sun."

He glanced down.

"I don't get what you're telling me, love."

"I saw that type of sun on a bloke's wall at the last scene we went to. The woman we nicked for it kept saying *it is the light* to me as well, and I've heard people say it since. None of it feels alright, sir."

He looked at her for a moment.

"Right, let me look into it. And in future – *two* sugar."

He returned to his papers. There was a long pause as she watched him pick up a well-chewed pencil and scribble on some documents before him.

"Leave to fall out, sir, please."

Wolfe scribbled for a second longer before his gaze idled up.

"Yes, yes, fall out."

Sheila stood up and made to open the door.

"And stop bloody well snooping, Sheel. There's a whole room of great big bleeders in there who'll do it for you."

She looked over her shoulder at him, but he was still in the middle of his papers. The door whined as she headed out of the office.

The bus trundled down Oxford Road through the rain as the city awoke. The newspaper vans absorbed all the pavement space they could, and the traffic moseyed past them. Pedestrians bottled themselves under any canopy available. The rain streaked across the bus windows like varicose veins. The bus was not as busy as normal, but the one ahead was full of people. Sheila had a month-old copy of *Amazing Stories* open at the story of that issue, *Professor Mainbocher's Planet.*

When the door opened, he found out — A pair of legs that would have broken up an octogenarian's convention — figure, face, and complexion to match — hazed eyes and high-lighted auburn hair.

Bloody hell, it's me, she thought. She peered over the top of the issue and saw a ragged man sat on the pavement next to the bus, bleary eyed and mouth in perpetual motion, as though chewing. He clocked eyes with Sheila and a yellow, interrupted grin erupted across his face. Sheila smiled back behind her magazine as he rolled around, reaching for a bottle of something as people sauntered past him. She couldn't help but giggle at his impromptu morning theatre. The bus drove past the Refuge building and towards St. Peter's Square. The Midland Hotel loomed into view. Sheila closed her magazine and rang the bell. The bus stopped opposite the cenotaph and she hopped off towards Anderson Street. The traffic died away and the pedestrians began to disappear as she made her way up the street. The rain got heavier, and the clouds got darker with every minute. She crossed the road, feeling the rainwater splash her shins and knees as she trotted across. She turned to Anderson Street and saw a group of Bobbies outside. As she got closer, she noticed more of them.

It looked like a fire drill or something similar had happened. The detectives were laughing and trying to light cigarettes while taking shelter under the previous day's edition of the *Evening News*. The rest of the company wore expressions that were at turns pensive and worried. There was an ambulance parked outside.

"Ee-arr, Sheila!" Fletcher shouted above the rain and the chatter. Sheila scanned the crowd and saw her, stood in an archway opposite the station, along with a group of other WPCs. Sheila went across to join them. When she got to them, they were ashen faced and looked terrified.

"Fletch?"

"Horror show, Sheel. Silly bloody paki topped herself in the cells last night. We found her just before morning parade."

There was a commotion on the steps of the station. The officers parted and a stretcher came down the steps. Sheila struggled to speak.

"But, she didn't look like she'd…"

"Kenworthy!"

Sheila turned to see the Inspector on the other side of the road. He looked like a gargoyle, his incensed expression unmoving in the battering rain, bottom teeth bared and eyes rifle slits in a parapet. All chatter died away in the archway. Sheila did not move for a second and then crossed the road. He took her by the arm and led her around the corner into the automotive yard. He swung her around to face him.

"Why did you bring her in?"

"Sir?"

"Under what charge did you bring that woman into our station, Sheila?"

"Assaulting a police officer, sir."

He stamped his foot and roared.

"Don't bloody well lie to me, constable! She, the last living relative, our only fucking witness to the murder of an entire bloody family, comes in and tops herself, because whoever supplied her blankets didn't have the good sense to take them away. The Desk Sergeant says she's meant to be in the drunk tank, Traffic say she's assaulted an officer, Desk Sergeant's unaware of any such charge and then, when I'm about ready to kill him, informs me that *you brought her in?* Am I correct, Kenworthy?"

Sheila could only bring herself to nod.

"Also, do you want to tell me about this?"

He produced a piece of paper from his pocket. It was crushed, but Sheila could see the drawings.

"That's Bibi Hussein's, sir..."

"Is it? Is it really? I bloody know it is, because I told you to bloody well take it back. Only you bloody well didn't. It landed on Wolfe's desk and then on mine. Don't get me wrong, we agree it's worth bugger all, but I still get a roasting because my Women's Officer's gone Agatha bloody Christie on me. Can't have it, cannot bloody have it. When we get back in that building, you're going straight back to Evidence and you'll stay there until you quit or you marry. Clear?"

The Inspector's words sprung back off the brickwork and faded into the rain.

"Yes, sir."

He cocked his head.

"The coroner's coming at some point. I'll handle it. Keep it shut."

He set off into the rain and turned the corner. She set on the step under the arch and put her head into her hands.

JKN250386, EMG020285, JMN280212, LEM020285, WJM040312, NMM091010, GAG280481...

Richardson's list stretched on like code. Some of his cases were getting heard at the Court of Appeals. He had known about them for months, but he asked for the evidence only now. He passed the sheet to Sheila, wordless and fleeting, in the bustle after morning parade and vanished before she could reproach him. Now it lay on her desk, already gathering dust and ash flakes from her cigarettes.

The basement felt cold. It felt as if the shelves held their gaze upward, refusing to look at her. Rodent feet itched and scratched the flooring somewhere in the gloom. The clock had stopped working, fixed at 5:37. Whoever had covered for her had not removed their mugs, which sat, half-drunk and white with scum, like open sores on her desk. Another one of the light fittings had come loose, so that only the bulb above her gave constant light.

She felt no urge to stand or do anything. She had lit and taken one drag from this cigarette but had not put it to her lips since. The ember – red, malevolent – made its millimetric way to her finger webbing. She watched it, willing it to go faster. It bit into her, searing as it went. Her hand shook and she clenched it into a fist, smoke running through her fingers. She locked her jaw and squeezed her teeth together. A small drop of blood ran across her knuckles.

With her other hand, she opened the desk drawer and removed the hairbrush. She rubbed her thumb across the hairs, and then pushed her way down to the bristles. She carried on going, feeling the bristles needle into her and force their way into the joint. A sob she had held back burst out of her mouth and pulled her whole body with it, jerking her with each breath.

There was a moment of stillness. She let the items fall to the floor. Congealed blood covered the cigarette butt like lipstick. Her skin had blistered into a deep red well. She pinched it with her other hand and twisted it until it burst, and she stifled a yelp in her closed mouth. When she opened her mouth, she felt her lungs wind up and her throat widen. She became louder and louder until she was screaming, eyes closed and face red. Her lungs began to ache, and the echoes died away.

Her muscles gave out and she slumped off the chair on to the floor. A cloud of grime and dust rose and settled on her tunic. Wheezing, she rolled onto her side. She caught sight of a rat scampering across from one shelf to another. The shelves and corridors remained impassive, swallowing light above the bulbs and beyond the parcels. A vast, indifferent silence followed.

She lay like this for what seemed like hours. Water pipes for the stations heating rattled across the ceiling. The grit, pressed into her face as she lay there, burrowed no deeper into her skin. She felt suspended off the ground and her breathing was heavy and slow. The door opened and a pair of feet clopped on the stone floor, sending shocks into her ear.

"Sheel?"

Sheila did not respond to Fletcher's voice. There were a couple more steps, when Fletcher gasped.

"Shit love, you alright? Bloody hell..."

Sheila felt Fletcher's tight grip on her tunic, but only moved her a couple of inches off the floor. Sheila rolled onto her back and faced Fletcher. She sat up and rubbed her face.

"Sorry, I fell off my chair." The words tumbled off Sheila's tongue like actors falling onto a stage. Fletcher looked at her through a disapproving squint.

"Chair, aye."

Fletcher took her by the hands and pulled her up. At that second, Gibbons turned into the room and took a step back.

"Kenworthy, what in God's name do you think you're made up as?"

"Sorry, Sergeant, I fell off my chair."

"You look like you've been rolling in the hay." Gibbons' eyes flashed to Fletcher, who let go of Sheila's hands and gave a reflexive shake of the head. Sheila brushed herself down.

"Just helping her up, Serg..."

"Kenworthy, where are those exhibits?"

Sheila pointed gingerly at the desk.

"There are some there, I'm just about to get the others."

Gibbons rolled her eyes.

"Ten minutes until parade, ladies." She walked away. Fletcher took hold of Sheila again by the arm.

"Stop acting strange, Sheel. They're already talking about sending you to Blakehill nick." Fletcher pulled Sheila closer to her and spoke to her, eye to eye.

"You're a mad one, you, but only I'm allowed to say that. There's nothing going on in Grandview, so relax." Sheila pulled away and turned her back.

"No. Some bastard burned a little girl and her whole family and no one gives a tuppence fuck about it."

"They clearly bloody do, Sheel, there's a room full of people trying to find out what fucker did it."

"Aye, and they're drinking a lot of tea and having a lot of laughs while it'll happen again. And it'll keep happening, because they'll do bugger all about it. They're a bloody shower of shite, up there, an absolute shower of shite. And you won't help as long as you're putting on your lippy and flicking your hair and blowing kisses at them like the thicko they want you be like, that they want us all to be like."

Fletcher stepped past Sheila and picked up the parcels on her desk.

"I'll take this to CID so you don't have to, if that's how you feel, Miss Marple." She made a headbutt move towards Sheila, like a snake. Sheila flinched, and Fletcher walked out of the room.

"Crack the case, then. I'll write to you in the loony bin, you daft cow," she called back.

Six

Rows of uniformed officers stood at ease while the Inspector read the bulletin. The parade square was in the middle of the building and only saw use at the start and end of the day. It was now dark, and the noises of the city soared over the courtyard. The detectives stood at the windows of the CID office, making faces and semaphore signals in an attempt to make the probationers laugh.

"...so, starting tomorrow, the Women's Officers are going to be on community outreach. There's a new boatload of them arriving every day, and we need to make sure that people don't resort to their baser instincts. And yes, I'm talking about you, territorial."

There was a low collective snigger in the ranks.

"Patrols as usual, no need to cancel leave yet. Just be a presence and be cheerful as ever. If you do happen to learn anything, then pass it on to your Sergeant." He turned to Gibbons, who saluted. They murmured to one another for a moment. Sheila tensed her arms, her left-hand tightening around her right wrist. She did not move, weathering a silent storm of judgement and ridicule from the ranks around her, hoping for the Inspector and Gibbons to dismiss them for the evening. All she could see were the backs and sides of people's heads, rows of buns or the short back and sides with a square neck, shielded by tall helmet, a cold and aloof court. A voice, speaking behind closed teeth, crept along her row.

"If you want your case ballsing up properly, notify Detective Kenworthy."

There were a couple of breathy, stifled laughs.

"Sheila Kenworthy, the paki slayer," came another. Someone cackled once, catching it before anyone could notice.

"Who fucking said that?" Sheila blurted out.

"Quiet in the ranks!" Gibbons barked. Her eyes scanned across the square for a second, before they paused on Sheila. She did not meet the look, but she felt it. Car bells sang out of the automotive yard and continued the next street over, joining a pair of car horns in a distant, atonal chorus. The Inspector stamped his heels and marched away. Gibbons gave the order to dismiss. The ranks took their steps and began to disperse. Sheila looked to her right and saw Gibbons coming towards her, head forward, her gait smooth and quick like something was reeling her in. Sheila came to attention as Gibbons stood before her, pointed at one constable, a lanky and thin-cheeked probationer, and beckoned him over. Those around him disappeared into the building without a word. He walked over, unsure of himself, and stood next to Sheila. Gibbons trained her flinty eyes on him for a moment and then focused on Sheila.

"Talk, constable." Gibbons' voice was softer than usual.

"I'm sorry, Sergeant..."

"I didn't tell you to apologise, Kenworthy, I told you to talk. What happened just then?"

"Sergeant…" the probationer began.

"Don't speak until I tell you to!" Gibbons bellowed. The man sank back into himself. Sheila continued.

"Nothing, Sergeant."

Gibbons sighed. Her voice was flat and bored.

"I am not matron, nor am I *Miss* Gibbons, Kenworthy. You've been here long enough to know how to conduct yourself on parade." She took a couple of steps until she was looking up at the probationer. "As for *you*, whatever your name is, you have been here nowhere near long enough and I can bore you to death with ease. Try me. If you wish to continue pratting about, then you'll be in support services, sweeping horse manure out of the stables. Understand?"

The probationer swayed a bit and his mouth opened to reply.

"Good. Go away, the pair of you."

As they walked off the square, a collective ghostly *oooh* came from CID, followed by drumming on the windows. Sheila left the door open and stepped inside.

The probationer leant his long body on the corridor wall, one leg cocked out to the middle of the floor and his head back a little. Sheila nudged the back of his knee, so he slipped down the wall and staggered backwards, and walked past him. He regained his footing and took bounding steps towards her as she made her way up the corridor.

"Oi, oi, you..."

Sheila carried on going. His steps came closer until he emerged at her side.

"Oi, that wasn't very nice of you, was it?"

Sheila turned to him and pushed him into the wall by his breastbone. His back met the wall like a book slamming shut.

"Oi? Bloody oi?"

"Get off me, dyke."

"Hey, you big gangly twonk, what the bloody hell have I ever done to you?"

He slapped her hand away and stepped over her, widening his eyes like a shark. Sheila bared her teeth and pushed her face into his.

"Go on, big brave boy, I bloody dare you..."

"Ee-arr, Sheila?" Fletcher's voice came down the corridor. The probationer's bearing shrank back. She looked over her shoulder at his tight expression and stretched her lips into an emotionless smile as she walked away. Fletcher stood at the top of a brief set of stairs, idly pulling a curl of hair from under her cap. Sheila frowned and jerked her head back in the probationer's direction.

"He's a git, isn't he?" She stated as she made her way over.

"Knobhead's union, you and him," Fletcher said. Her eyes had a knowing softness around them.

"Come on, Fletch, we can't be like this."

"*You* come on, Sheel, I were being dead nice in Evidence and you were bit of a prick to me. *Sorry, Fletch. You're welcome, Sheel.*"

Sheila dropped her head.

"Sorry, Fletch."

"No worries. And I like wearing lippy, so shut your face."

They made their way to Evidence. Sheila took her coat and made her way to leave.

"Sheel, where's your relief?" Fletcher asked. Sheila stopped and groaned.

"Don't make me stay here on me todd, Fletch."

"And you're having a laugh if you think I'm staying here a second longer, love."

"Right, I'll come with you to CID while you get your belongings, then?"

"And risk Gibbo giving you the duty talk?"

"Yeah, I'll go batty down here on me own." Sheila hunched her back and dragged her foot behind her, making limping steps towards Fletcher. *"Bringeth me a golden goat's gonad, and I'll tell ye fortune!"* She cackled as Fletcher rolled her eyes.

"Fine, fine, fine, come up. Silly cow."

They arrived at CID, where the men sat around a radio. Crowd noise, commentary and longwave static roared at full volume, like air rushing through a gap in a huge set of teeth. Those who stood around the office were swore at one other and everyone seemed to have a drink of something strong. Sheila and Fletcher moved past the men like house help and found Fletcher's desk away from the men.

"Thank God City are away, traffic'd be a nightmare," Sheila said. Fletcher didn't respond as she took her coat and then began looking over the desk. Her head began to bob as though she was avoiding punches.

"Where's me shagging bag?" Fletcher grumbled. She dropped to her knees and reached under her desk. At that moment, Sheila noticed an open notebook on the desktop. Sheila took it and hid it under her coat.

"Got you, you little bastard" Fletcher hissed. She pushed herself back and stood up. They both walked out of the room, amid the gasps and shouts over the radio, and made their way downstairs at a quick pace. Fletcher turned around as they reached the front lobby, threw her head back, widened her eyes and reached out Sheila.

"Are you going to walk me home, then, sir?" Fletcher lisped.

"Get stuffed, Fletch."

Fletcher chuckled and stood straight, almost clicking her heels together.

"See you tomorrow, then."

Sheila set off to the basement, imagining Gibbons'
presence in her peripheral vision the whole way down. She
approached the single door at the bottom of the stairs and
opened it. The lights were on and there was no one in there.
She put her elbow on the desk and stretched her back. The
dismal basement was silent except for the odd thumping noise
from inside the pipes running across the ceiling. Her breathing
had an echo and the air was stagnant and damp. She looked
down at her desk. A note, written on a peach index card, sat on
top of the clutter.

You and I will be having words before morning
parade.

Sheila closed her eyes and took a deep breath.

"Evening love," the constable said, strolling past her
and behind the desk. He sat down, leant forward and laughed
a couple of times.

"She's omnipresent, int she?" he said, "She's the bloody
wrath of God, her."

"She's like Bovril, and most people hate Bovril."

"Aye, so you say. G'night," he half-slurred, before reaching into his pocket and producing a pack of player's medium. Sheila left the building.

The bus shelter rattled under the rain. Traffic headlights cut through the downpour like huge, searching antennae across the tarmac. Sheila took off her cap and flicked her wrist a couple of times to get the water off. She replaced the cap and took the notebook from under her coat. She turned the cover over and read the first entry on the page.

Lillian Chapman. Wythenshawe Hospital – ACU. Unreliable. The bus pulled up. Sheila got on.

An old couple were the only ones on the bus aside from Sheila as they approached Wythenshawe Hospital. It came to a halt and they all stood up. The old couple shuffled, the woman guiding the man by the arm as he coughed and coughed. She stepped off behind them into the sheen of evening rain. The approach to the front was not lit, but the buildings had a prominent silhouette from the city lights to the north. She carried on walking and more came into view. Orange light glinted off the scaffolding around the new buildings. They flanked the facade of the old sanatorium building, tarpaulin swinging in the breeze. She made her way through the huge brass-handled doors and walked inside. She followed the signs to the Acute Care Unit. Everything was new and clean. Each footstep reverberated to the point where there were multiple pairs of feet walking down the bereft corridors. She turned onto a concourse between the old and new buildings.

The strip lightbulbs were so bright that the concourse windows appeared black. Her reflection repeated itself in the windows opposite as she made her way to the ACU. Copy after copy of herself, stretched on into infinity like wings. The lights got brighter as she walked to the point where she was squinting. She looked to her left and saw a faceless reflection of herself. Her hair looked platinum in the light and she reached to touch it. She brought a curl down in front of her eyes. It was brown. She looked at herself again, and her hair had returned to itself. She could see her face again.

The ACU door opened.

"Excuse me, are you lost?" The nurse's lush Accrington lilt was enough to put anyone at ease.

"No, Nurse. I need to see one of your patients. A Mrs...Chapman?"

The nurse frowned.

"I'm not sure you want to."

"I won't be long, nurse. I'm just checking on her."

"Fine. This way."

They entered the ward. The patients sat up, reading or staring into space, in casts or behind pale masks. But the nurse took her past them and to a room, closed off, at the end of the ward. Sheila looked through the glass and caught her breath.

"We tried to transfer her to Springfield, but they won't have her until she heals. Every time she's unsecured, she hurts herself again or rips her bandages off. She's here for the foreseeable."

Sheila looked closer at Lillian, fastened to the bed by leather straps. It seemed as if she was not a living person, but a corpse kept animate by machines. Wounds tailed out from underneath her face mask, as if it had welded to her flesh. A few of her fingers were missing. Scars of deep scratches and lacerations traced across any uncovered flesh. Her breath was deep and quick.

"Has she said anything to anyone?"

"When she isn't screaming or trying to take a chunk out of you, she babbles all kinds of stuff."

"Like what?"

"She said lots of stuff about *light*. Couldn't get her to make any sense. Thought she was a bit sensitive, you know, because of the new lights we've got put in. But she said it no matter what. The room could have been pitch black and if you were in the room with her, she started wailing about *light this* and *light that*." The nurse shivered. Sheila put her hand on the nurse's shoulder.

"Is there anything you can remember, in particular? What she says?"

"Well, its not much, but she said *it is the light* all the time. I've asked her. Believe me, she just said it louder and then she started gnashing her teeth. She's chewed holes through her cheeks, you know."

"Pardon me, *said*? Is she not speaking any more?"

The nurse looked over both her shoulders.

"Not exactly. She bit her own tongue off a few days ago. Still doesn't stop her chatting."

"Christ almighty."

"Aye. She's gone doolally, bless her."

"I know. Interviewed her at the scene, got nothing out of her then."

The nurse faced Sheila. The light from the concourse shimmered in the corners of her eyes, which were like polished concrete. Sheila put her mouth the nurse's ear.

"Is it alright if I go in?"

"No, not at this time, the sister'll feed me to the dogs…"

There was a moan from inside the room. Sheila looked over and saw Lillian convulsing on the bed. The drip stand swayed and her saline drip came off its hook. She was taking deeper and deeper breaths until she forced herself upright. Her mask came away on the left side. Her eye was missing and there was a deep gash in her face which stretched from her eye socket to the corner of her mouth. She began screaming, but they were shielded by the door. Only the pitch of the note got through, and they felt her volume punch the door and bounce off. Her mouth was wide enough to reveal her tonsils and missing teeth. The rear of her tongue, jagged and abrupt, pulsed like a living cliff face. There were more scratches, fainter than the main injury, which stretched from her vacant eye. It was an annihilating reminder of Bibi's drawings. Of the man's wall.

"Come this way, constable. She'll just carry on like that."

They left the ward and regrouped at the front desk.

"Sorry about this, constable. She's hard work."

"It's alright, you can only do what you can. Are you sure she didn't mention anything else?"

The nurse's eyes rolled up as she mined anything of us.

"Aye, I'm sure. She's just bonkers."

"She said summat to me, you know," came a voice out of an ante room. There was another nurse, sat down with a cup of tea, leaning out and eavesdropping.

"Ee-arr, Debbie, are you being a nosey moo as per?"

"Nosey moo yourself, Joan, I'm helping here!"

Sheila leant against the front desk.

"What did she say?"

"Screamed *broken man, broken man* at me. Thought it were just her having a dig, but, you know, thought I'd tell."

Sheila smiled at her.

"Thanks, love."

"Ee, no problem, constable. Is it true, though? That she killed her family and that?"

"Debs, shut your gob!" The nurse hissed.

"We're not sure. Thank you anyway, for your time."

Sheila pushed the doors open to the ward and made her way across the concourse back to the old sanatorium. Silence and polite echoes met her steps. She looked left and right as she made her way down, to see what was happening in the wards. There were doctors, nurses, auxiliaries and other staff making their rounds as she walked. Wherever she walked, she seemed to get someone's attention and lock eyes with them. These people were not already passing by the windows and, it seemed to her, all were engrossed in something else. It was as if they had become aware of her presence by instinct and, until they lost sight of her, could not look away.

The lights were intense and repellent and, again, she squeezed her eyes until they were just open, trying to find any reprieve from the brightness. She carried on walking, now barely able to see the trolleys and chairs at the corridor's sides. The red linoleum walkway was the only thing guiding her to the exit. The great doors' dark windows, like pools of deep water, appeared at the end of her walk. She flung them open and stepped into the night. Residual glare crept around her eyes as she looked back at the hospital.

She was not sure what it was, or if it was even there. She could not tell if there was a shape at the window, or if she was still partly blinded. The caustic, throbbing glare made it hard to tell.

She walked to the bus, idling in the bay. The engine's chugging rhythm made the whole vehicle vibrate. She sat down and opened the book. She knew where to find the *broken man.*

19 Ogwen Street

Grandview

Seven

The demolition ball hung from the crane like a rotten cherry. It swung in the collecting wind. Rain flayed the ground with each gust over the rooftops. The houses either side of where the burned house used to be were now huge piles of brick, pale and exposed like skinned flesh. No lights appeared in any of the windows opposite. The houses stood derelict, cleared during the week, and waiting to be levelled. The pavement Sheila stood on felt like the eye of the storm, as the wind and rain passed overhead like a huge waterfall.

She paced up the street towards the house where she had first met the man, hoping to find anything she could use. The streetlights were out at this end of the road and the windows were already smashed in. She arrived at the house and saw the door tilting off its hinges. The burgundy paint stopped at the door's borders, which had remained hidden by the doorframe until recently. It fell off completely as Sheila touched it to move it out of her way. It tumbled into the street like it was glad to escape. The stairs were visible and nothing else. Her hand ran up the wall leading to the front room and she turned into it, feeling debris underfoot.

She took another step and felt a large crack under foot, which made her jump. She brushed the floor with her other foot and heard the tinkling and dumb roll of an empty bottle. The light came through the gap in the blackout curtains like amber on black velvet. She threw them open, rank smelling dirt and dust flying off in grey clouds, and turned around.

Whoever had come in after the man left had taken the carpet, light fittings and anything else that could be stripped. A draught crawled across her body from the rear door. The corner she stood next to stank of piss. She walked towards the chimney breast and stared hard at it. The pattern was untouched. Circle pattern, torn into the wallpaper. A dot in its centre. Strips surrounding it. Crude, yet it burst out of the dark and dominated the room, everything else indistinguishable in the dark. She ran her hand over the torn wallpaper. It felt stiff over her fingers as they went. She brushed a layer of dust off the mantelpiece once she reached the bottom. She felt a series of lumps and ridges, like the back of a beetle, which interrupted the gloss paint. She drew her hand back and pushed it over again, feeling the engraving's contours. She opened her bag and fumbled, finding a tissue and a pencil. She placed the tissue on the mantelpiece and began to brush the pencil over it.

There was a razor thin creak from the kitchen. Sheila felt her heart vault against her ribs and she dropped the pencil, which rattled like a shell casing. The worktop next to the door was just visible and nothing else. Her body trembled as she sank to one knee and pawed at the ground for anything to wield. She lifted the lid of her bag with her other hand and stuffed the tissue inside. An edge of broken glass purred as it scraped against her. She pinched it and held it up, careful not to press it into her palm, and held it in front of her. Still in a crouch, she pulled her skirt higher than her knee and inched towards the kitchen, clamping her mouth shut over her teeth to keep herself quiet. Raindrops began hitting the rear windows harder and faster as she arrived at the doorway. She stepped into the kitchen, keeping the shard in front of her, as though trying to cut the air. She stopped. The kitchen remained silent.

A step sounded on the rear garden on the flagstones, grinding across errant gravel like a clearing throat. A quick series of steps followed. Sheila dropped the glass and ran into the garden. Something, enshrouded in the dark, scrambled over the back wall and took off up the rear alley. Sheila wrestled with the rusty rear gate bolt and shoved it back into its housing. She threw it open and looked left and right up the alley. It was pointless in the suffocating dark and she stood a moment in the rain, removing her cap and shaking her head.

She took a step back into the house from the rear yard and looked at the floor. She could not see the glass shard she had dropped. There was an expectant stillness inside, as if the house was holding its breath. She turned on her heel and ran into the alley. She turned towards the top of the street, towards the light and where she hoped there would be no gate.

She looked behind herself as she ran and could not see behind her. She could not see below her waist. A bar, or some kind of metal debris in the alley, caught her ankle as she ran and for a split second she flew towards the ground, before colliding with the old cobble stones.

In the space of a blink, the alley was illuminated. Sheila lifted her head from the floor, which looked fresh and clean, and there was no trash. The sky was a deep and luminous blue, as if lightning had been frozen in the middle of a strike in the night sky. The streetlights were the colour of fool's gold in the idle mist. She turned again and headed for where she thought the figure may have gone. She could see a house on her left. There was a small alley next to it. It was a complete black, an enormous void, swallowing the light from the street. She approached it and looked into the pregnant darkness. She couldn't feel the wind or hear any of the sounds that made up the evening streets. The dark appeared almost opaque. She reached into the darkness. It fell apart around her hand. Something scratched against her legs.

The floor was alive, bubbling, with rats. She dry heaved as the train of rodents moved through her legs and over her feet before arcing into the fog beyond. Mud and tears from their claws covered her tights. Dots of blood emerged on her shin like eyes. She felt a pressure in her head and cupped her face in her hands. When she removed them, something was obscuring her vision.

It looked like glass blades, or another set of eyelashes. She put her hands up to her eyes and pulled. Strands of hair, blonde, golden and glistening, were in her hands. She searched for the roots. She pulled again and felt her vision blur. Then again, seeing the pale red of her eyelids. Now she yanked the hair, pulling it out in great bunches, but each time the hair invaded her sight. Her hands began to scratch at her face, until she was clawing at her eyes.

There was a sudden glare. The street light gathered and emerged in an enormous mass above her head. The white, oppressive light shone down the alley.

There were children stood in a circle. At first, it resembled a council initiative to *welcome your immigrant neighbours*. Flanked by sultry red brickwork and looking ahead, they wore summer dresses or striped shirts bow ties. They stood with nondescript, baby-toothed smiles. Bibi was among them. There was a low sound, as if a great door had slammed shut in the distance. As one, they looked up and their eyes widened. Their happiness dripped away into a terrified stillness. They collapsed into brace positions and covered their heads, all facing towards the centre of their circle.

Their clothes ignited in blue flame and their skin began to scorch. She couldn't smell the burning of leather, of fabric, of skin, but she knew it was there. It had a presence of its own. Flame rolled over carbonised skin, hungry for new flesh to consume. Their hands burnt around heads, detonating hair. Then, as if practised, their hands reached out, in unison, to the centre of their circle. Each body stretched to reach the centre before slowing to a stop. Black skin became grey ash, flaking in the numbed breeze. They had disintegrated into piles of nothing and these piles moved together to form a hill. The almighty glare reassembled above the ash. A brilliant orb, surrounded by thin beams of annihilating light.

The light dimmed to nothing.

"Ee-arr, do you think she's dead?"

The voices were distant and were unsteady.

"Get her bag, go on."

There was a tugging under her arm and the flap hit her back. After a brief period of rustling, her keys fell on the floor next to her. She moved her head and took a gulp of air. The dirt scraped against her face from the floor.

"Shit, shit, run!"

Their footsteps clattered away into the alley like rocks falling down a cliff side. Laughing, young, carefree and cruel, sounded around the corner before fading into the night. Propping herself up on one arm, she felt the weight of the blow she had received pull her back to the ground. She turned her head and the weight rolled with her like ballast in her head. When she opened her eyes, she saw it was still night, but only just. The rain had stopped, but she was soaked and shook in the cold. Wet coat and wet tunic weighed her down and each effort to get up was immense. The outline she left on the ground was pale in the dawn. She touched her face. Pain and heat stabbed at her head and shoulders and she cried out. She brought her hand to her face again and braced herself. The wound was small, but deep. There was a little blood. Yet the whole right side of her face was swollen and pushed against her skull. Touching the inside of her cheek with her tongue made her head feel like it would come apart. Her right eye would not open. She rolled herself back onto her knees and felt around for her bag. It was open and she could not find her purse. She carried on, pushed her hand around as if to push through the leather. A ball of coarse tissue pressed against her palm and she let it go, pressing it flat into the bottom. She drew her hand out and closed the flap. After scrambling for her keys, she got to her feet and made her way down the streets back.

She inched up the stairs as Alice snored like a diesel engine in the front room. Her legs began to stiffen with pain from the distance she had walked. With one shoulder, she pushed through her door and held the edge with one hand to quieten it as it closed. She dropped her coat and prised off her clothes. Her knees were grazed and her arms were bruised. Her skin seemed pale to the point of translucent. She took her washing bowl, went downstairs and boiled the kettle. It started to whistle after a minute. She took it off the stove and poured it into the bowl. She took the bowl and began to tread back to her room. She looked and saw that Alice had gone. She carried on up the stairs.

She got to her room and wrapped herself up. Every splash of water her face removed the dirt of ages and stung her sharper. By the time she had finished, she felt as if her face did not belong to her and that it was angry about the fact. She sat on her bed and placed her feet in the bowl. She spat a thick and bloody glob of something into her mouth, swallowed it and coughed a little. A minute passed, and she looked up into her mirror.

The face she saw reminded her of an earlier one. Framed by an iron lung, like a grotesque bust. Mouth hanging slightly and one side of the face bulging, a nest filled with black blood. The other side untouched, the whole face a timeline of destruction. Head shaved of blonde hair.

She looked away and took her bag. She flipped it open and felt around for the tissue. It was in the corner, bunched together and damp. She held it in her hand and saw it protrude through her fingers like limestone. Her fingers loosened their grip and she separated the pieces like a fruit skin, examining them one by one in the dimness.

She found it the one. The pencil lead had bled from the water and almost nothing remained. But there was one word. Twisted, shaded and boxy, from a crude carving. A curious word. If a word at all.

Aakeran.

Eight

Looks of all kinds – from sideways glances to immobilising
stares – latched onto Sheila from all sides as she walked into
Anderson Street, head down and pace quick. Her right eye had
only started to reopen, and her right cheek was a sickly,
bubonic violet. She had a magazine in one hand and half
raised it over her face, but knew that she was attracting
attention either way.

"Sheel?" Fletcher's voice sounded dryer than normal.
Sheila carried on walking towards the basement. She heard
Fletcher's footsteps increase in pace and match hers, a little
behind her. They both entered the stone staircase to the
basement, which was empty.

"Sheel, you alright? What happened to you?"

"Tell you in a bit, Fletch."

"Oh no you bloody won't."

Fletcher put her hand on Sheila's shoulder. Sheila
yelped and pulled away from Fletcher's hand. She looked up
and stopped.

"Oh Christ, love, sorry....Jesus wept, Sheel."

They stood for a moment.

"Should see the other bloke, ha ha ha."

"What're you going to tell Gibbo?"

Sheila shrugged and was about to reply.

"Kenworthy, down here, please."

Fletcher pulled a face and left the stairs. Sheila went down the stairs and down the basement corridor. She entered the basement and Gibbons was standing there with her back to the door.

"Let's get this over with, then." Gibbons began, before turning around.

"Sheila, I don't know how long I can...oh my god." Sheila stood there and folded her lips back in a knowing manner. Gibbons' demeanour changed for a moment, betraying her concern and shock, before hiding behind her stony expression. It was a brief time before Gibbons spoke.

"Dare I ask?"

"I fell, Sergeant."

Gibbons stepped forward and turned Sheila's face to the side with a gentle push of her forefinger. It felt like the muzzle of a pistol.

"Right. Have you been to see the medic?"

"No, Sergeant."

Gibbons let go of Sheila's face and their gaze found one another again.

"Sorry about last night, Sergeant, I was in dereliction of duty as a constable..."

"Bugger last night, come upstairs, let's get looked at. Don't abandon your post again."

Gibbons took Sheila by the underarm, who did not protest as they went upstairs. They made their way down the middle of the station's corridors as the rest of the officers made their way to morning parade. Sheila felt like a rock in the middle of a stream, conscious of the slowing footsteps and murmurs around her. She hung her head a little and kept up with Gibbons.

They carried on until they were in a far corner of the station, where the brickwork stood unpainted. There was a small room which could be heard before it could be seen. Eddie Calvert's *Oh Mein Papa*, screaming out what should have been serene, on an ancient, pocket turntable. They approached the room and Gibbons knocked on. The door opened and a tired man in a dishevelled police uniform emerged. His skin veered between yellow and green and his eyes hid themselves as far back as they could inside his head. Sheila wasn't sure if the white armband he wore, adorned with the red cross, was meant to mark him as a medic or as an invalid.

"What can I do you for?" he gurgled, before coughing up a chunk of phlegm.

"Meredith, can you attend to Sheila please?" Gibbons asked. He stood for a second and looked at Sheila, who still had her head down. She saw the cigarette butts scattered all over the floor, lying like casualties on a battlefield. Meredith's throat scratched again.

"I mean, I will, but I'm not Jesus, or owt..."

He stepped forward and made to lift Sheila's head. She saw his tar-stained, hastily bitten fingers and looked up before he had the chance to touch her. He drew his hand back and stepped closer to her.

"When did this happen, Gibbo?"

Sheila felt the lack of response like an extra atmosphere. She could hear Gibbons' blood begin to simmer.

"*Sergeant*, Meredith. And sometime last night. Can we get this sorted, please?"

Meredith winked at Sheila.

"Absolutely, Gibbo. C'mere, love, let's get you looked at."

Gibbons let go of her, and the door closed behind her. Sheila sat down on a leather padded chair, which looked as if it had been chewed, and he took a seat opposite her.

"To be completely honest, I'm not sure that I can do much for you, my darling. Can give you a few minutes doing naff all, though, if you want." He turned the legs of his chair, hopping on the concrete floor, to a small table. There was a large Spanish onion, sitting like an antique grenade, on top of some papers. He began to peel the onion skin with his calloused thumb.

"Who gave you that then? You can tell me, patient's confidence and all that." He continued pulling the skin away from the onion bulb, which started to fragment as his nails caught it.

"I really fell. I was running, I tripped up and smacked my face on the floor." Sheila felt guilty saying these words, even though it was the truth.

"Aye, did the floor get angry about not getting its dinner? Or 'cos you talked back?" He held up the onion and studied it, before smirking in appreciation at his handiwork.

"No, definitely fell. Smacked me face. Now it hurts. A lot."

He turned to her and half smiled.

"You'll have a shiner for a couple of days, but your face'll be less puffy tomorrow, like." He took a hearty bite out of the onion, which oozed down his chin. He kept eye contact with her as he rolled the food around his half-open mouth. Sheila felt her nostrils begin to curl open and he swallowed his food.

"Think what you like, love, but I'm Manchester's Popeye and this is my spinach. Make you into ten men, one of these." He bit into it again and continued to speak. "Provost Sergeant at Aldershot kept an arm's length away from me, you know. And he was a big handy bastard, believe me. Just knew that I could have ripped his arms off and picked me teeth with them, I tell thee." A piece of onion fell out of his mouth with his final word. Sheila looked away and held back a laugh.

"Aye, yes. Terrifying..." she began.

"Ey, you, look at me when you're taking the piss." He had his eyebrows raised as if he meant to expel them off his face.

"Yes, Meredith." Sheila twisted her mouth to stop smiling. He leant in.

"That, and my bloody breath could have taken his head off."

Sheila's forced its way through her rasping her lips as he revealed his craggy, tanned-tooth smile. He sat back and carried on munching, flexing his left bicep.

"Try it somewhere else, Meredith. I'm not in that kind of a mood."

"Same as every other woman, love. Don't worry, don't give a shit." He placed the half-eaten onion on the table and wiped his face with the back of his sleeve.

"You the one from the basement, yeah?"

Sheila rolled her eyes.

"Yes."

"Only asking, love. I heard about what happened. Sorry about all that, it's not fun when someone dies on you." He reached into his tobacco tin and began rolling. "Was it your first time?"

"I'm sorry?"

"Your first death, love. Was that your first?"

"Oh, no. Didn't mean for her to die, you know."

Meredith regarded her with a quizzical look.

"Well, we know that much. But you can't stop someone doing something stupid like that, you know. If someone wants to go, they just go." He licked along the paper and sealed his cigarette. "We had lads in Crete that could have made a full recovery, if they'd wished. But then they'd only end up going to some kraut shit hole in Poland instead of being the *gallant dead*." He shrugged and lit his cigarette with the smouldering end of a dying one from his ashtray.

"Her whole family died. Can't say I blame her if she wanted to go."

"Really? Jesus, all the way from Bengal for something like that to happen. Poor girl. You been alright?"

"As well as I can be, yeah. Still got a roof over my head, like."

They sat for a second while he took a long drag and blew it into the air like a searchlight.

"I don't understand, though. She just wanted to go to sleep when I left her," Sheila said, "She gave it beans to me, I tell you that."

"Hmm."

"She said that there were people who wanted to get her in here," Sheila said.

He began coughing, each hack making the cigarette jump in his mouth.

"You're pulling my leg if you think she was knocked. Do you really think so?"

"I don't know, Meredith. I can't have it all end with her, though."

"Don't look for an answer where there isn't one, love. Everyone she knows dies and then she ends up in a cell. Like it wouldn't cross your mind?" He took another drag and looked at her with an expression that betrayed the sadness of one who knew. Sheila nodded and rubbed her jawline where she felt a throbbing.

"How did you know where she was from?" she murmured.

"Death certificate, love. I had to sign it."

"Ah, right."

He picked up the onion and began eating again. He looked into the middle distance and shook his head with incredulity at the memory he was reliving.

"Nearly broke that probationer's neck, though. Scrawny bastard bendover made a paki joke as they were cutting her down."

"The big blonde one, with the slappable face?"

"Aye, and you're a kind one, just giving him a slap. I said I'd twist him in a figure-eight knot and he damn nearly wet himself."

"Where can I find him?"

"I hope you're not going to send him here with broken knees?"

Sheila forced an airy laugh.

"No, just curious. Had a run-in with him after last evening parade."

Meredith's neck straightened. He pointed his finger at her.

"Did he..."

"No, no, no, I would have killed him if he tried anything like this. What's he called?"

He dropped his finger and sat back into his chair, taking another drag on the nub of the cigarette.

"Butterwick."

"Bugger off. Seriously?"

"Yep. He's on Sergeant Garrett's beat near Albert Square while they take his stabilisers off. Wants to be in territorial. I'd have an easier time getting into the House of Lords."

Sheila smiled and felt a stab of pain in her cheek, which made her cringe and hold her face. He stood up.

"Do you want some ice for that?"

Sheila nodded. He left the room. The 45 had finished, and the needle kept scratching and bumping against the record's edge.

A burst of laughter erupted from a table occupied by traffic officers, quietening the canteen for a brief moment. Heads turned over from the queue and then continued with their conversations or stared into space. The food smelled better than it looked – flaky sandwiches, dark tea and square shaped cakes with grey custard. Conversation carried on across the room, bawdy jokes and station gossip existing alongside talks of the Sergeant's exam and upcoming prosecutions. They ate off plates with odd patterns, added to the canteen over several years. All this took place over mismatched tablecloth. Garish floral prints, bright gingham, fading white, all bearing ancient stains like lesions.

Sheila kept the cold compress against her face. The ice had long melted, but the bag shielded her face from other people's looks. The dinner ladies behind the counter looked like siblings. Tight, curly hair, behind black hair nets, faint moustaches and manic, corporate laughter as they rushed and busied about in the kitchen. Sheila picked up a plate with sandwiches on and made to carry on.

"Eee, what happened to you?"

Sheila made to reply, only for the woman to interrupt her again.

"Don't tell me, you were scrapping with some ne'er-do-well and he got you?"

Sheila closed her eyes and got half a sound out before the woman carried on.

"Bank robber? Manchester's most wanted? I knew it, you're a one, aren't you?"

Sheila beamed at the woman who passed over a cup of tea. Sheila put the bag down and took the cup, balancing it on the edge of her plate.

"Bloody nora, did a right number on you there, didn't he? Don't worry about paying, love - my treat!"

"Oh, cheers, thanks!" Sheila replied, placing the bag on her face and adopting a debutante's floating walk as she went with her lunch. There was a small amount of muttering at a table behind her.

"How come she doesn't get to pay?" jabbered an outraged, muffled voice. Sheila looked and saw Butterwick, his hand outstretched, his cheeks stuffed and flecked by pastry.

"Some Man United supporter's given her a black eye and we don't stand for that in my canteen!"

A table nearby thumped their table in appreciation. Sheila made it over to Fletcher's table, who was shaking her head and smiling.

"You're bloody terrible, you," Fletcher said.

"Aye, but I'm gorgeous," Sheila replied, pulling a face and taking a bite out of her sandwich. She looked over at Butterwick, who finished his food in one mouthful, forced it back and stood up in indignation, making his cutlery jangle.

"Paki lover," he spat. The same nearby table made a girlish noise and began laughing. He turned to storm out, but a man with sergeant's stripes grabbed him by the wrist, pulled him down to ear level and whispered hurried words. He let go, and Butterwick sloped out. Sheila looked at Fletcher, who had her tongue in her cheek.

"True love, eh?" Fletcher droned.

"Sooner become a nun, like your mum."

"My mum's well classier than you, Sheel."

The sergeant stood up at Butterwick's table and walked over to Sheila. She recognised him as Garrett. His eyes pierced out from drooping eyelids like a landmine fuse.

"Come with me a minute, love, finish your dinner in a bit." He stood back as Sheila got up. She turned, unsure of what would happen, and walked out of the canteen and into the corridor, which was empty aside from a pacing Butterwick. Garrett raised his hand up to chest level, two fingers aloft like a saint's painting. Butterwick stopped and seemed to fall back into himself.

"Apologise to the women's constable, probationer," Garrett ordered.

He looked at Sheila's legs and brushed his hair back with one hand, before looking away again. Garrett stepped forward and leant in, pressing Butterwick's face against the wall with his forehead.

"Do it, new boy."

"Sorry, women's constable," he bleated.

"Louder," Garrett directed. Sheila felt an unwelcome pang of sympathy lurch in her chest. She felt as if she was looking into the youth's recent past, as if he had swapped one corridor ritual for another.

"Sorry, women's constable!" he squawked.

"That's women's constable *Kenworthy!*" Garrett yelled. Sheila took a step forward, but Garrett raised his hand and she backed off.

"Sorry, women's constable Kenworthy!" Butterwick cried. A couple of officers up the corridor stared at the exchange. Garrett took a breath and composed himself, looking more like a man and less of animal about to strike. He looked over at Sheila.

"Settled?"

"Yes, Sergeant."

"Good. On you go, love."

She turned around and walked back into the canteen. Faces looked away from the door, although every ear still attended to her entrance. Fletcher took a mug away from her lips and sat up. Sheila took her seat and picked up her sandwich as if it were a foreign artefact, not knowing if she should eat it or not. There was little sound for a moment. As Fletcher was about to speak, a series of deadened barks and shouts came through the wall and the gossiping around the tables began. A moment later those nearest the doors anchored their attentions on their plates. The door did not burst open, rather it opened on a slow and deliberate turn. Garrett entered with a ghoulish walk and made his way over to Sheila's table. He put his hand on her shoulder and patted twice, before walking back to his table and taking his seat.

"Good on him. Give him the boot up the arse he needs."

"Aye. Come on, Fletch, Gibbo'll be round in a couple of minutes.

They finished their lunch and walked out of the canteen. Butterwick was still standing on the other side of the corridor, brushing himself down and looking up.

"Bloody wet bag, him. Want me to come down to the basement, Sheel?"

"I'll be alright, thanks."

Sheila made her way downstairs and opened the door. She walked over to the travelling stove and turned it on. She examined her distorted reflection in the side of the old steel kettle. A figure, no more than a smudge appeared to her right. It grew larger, until eventually she make out the smear of an eye and a stretched nose. Then the hair. Blonde. She turned around.

"Sheila?"

"Can I help you, Butterwick?"

He wrung his hands together and had an altogether younger appearance. He looked as if he was before the headmaster.

"Did I get your name right - Sheila?"

"You did. What do you want?"

"I came down to apologise. I'm really sorry for how I was up there."

"You've already bloody apologised, what're you on about?"

"I'm just trying to do the right thing."

"You're a twat, new boy. And I don't like twats. Anything else?"

"Excuse me, from what I hear, you're a big fan of twat, are you not?"

Sheila stepped around him and went to open the door.

"Listen here, you bad-mouthed little shit. What if I was to tell your mum how you speak to girls? Or, better yet, how about I go and drag Garrett out of his dinner so he can discuss it with you, yeah?"

His head shook to the point of trembling and his pupils constricted to near nothing.

"Oh give over..." Sheila said, but then he began to gasp for air. His face turned red and then began to darken. His eyes were streaming with tears. He proceeded to fall apart in front of her, dropping to his knees and then hitting his head on the stone floor. She rushed to his side and slapped his face.

"Butterwick? Wake up! Can you hear me?"

She hit him on the chin and it stung her hands. His eyes opened and he took a deep breath. He made to push himself up, but his arms wobbled and gave way. Rolling onto his right side, he starting weeping, coughing on a mouthful of dirt. The kettle began to whistle.

"Do you want a brew, Butterwick?"

He nodded through his sobs.

Nine

The chair Butterwick sat on creaked at his smallest movement. He clasped his hands around the mug of tea Sheila had given him. His tears, on reddened eyes, mingled with the steam, giving his eyes the look of a mural on a wet wall.

"Can I get you anything?" She asked, putting her hand on his forearm. He looked up, his hair was darkened by sweat.

"No, you're alright. Thanks for this." He sipped his drink with overly-pursed lips.

"Want me to bring Meredith down?"

"No, thanks. He'd have me doing what you're doing."

She carried on moving around the room, carrying disordered piles of parcels around, pretending to sort them.

"What was that all about?"

"Dunno. Sorry, again."

"Stop apologising. Has that happened to you before?"

"Aye, happened in Malaya, but I just said it was a fever. Being here terrifies me sometimes."

"Oh, come on, Garrett isn't *that* bad."

"And you'd know, why exactly?"

"Jesus, Butterwick, we do the same job, but you've done your national service. Don't tell me that you can't take a bollocking."

He half-laughed, and she heard him running his hands over his face.

"They dished it out, but at least they cared. Garrett just yells at me and tells me I'm always doing things wrong. If I try and be soft with a suspect, he barges me out the way and screams at them. If I try being loud, he shoves me back and then he turns into the Pope. I swear, it's impossible to be a copper around him."

Sheila turned and looked at him with scorn.

"Oh, boo bloody hoo. That's policing, good cop, bad cop. Get over yourself."

He threw his cup past Sheila's head, which made her drop the exhibits. It left a trail of tea on the floor and it shattered behind her. His eyes welled and his bottom teeth stuck out in infantile rage.

"Is it? Is it really? When he takes me to one side and screams at me when the Inspector tells me I've done a good job? Or gets in my face when my shoelace is untied, or I walk out of step when we're on the beat? When he laughs at me when I'm rolling around trying to cuff some drunk dosser, or when he threatens me after I've helped him cuff his? I do this fucking job because I want to help, to hit villains hard, and I get shat on every minute of every fucking day and I hate it, I hate it, I hate it!"

He started crying again. Sheila felt uneasy on her feet. She took a step forward towards him and then paused as he took control over himself.

"I told him I wanted to get into territorial and he just said I shouldn't even be a copper. I swear, some days I'd rather go back to Kedah and take my chances against chinks in the bushes." He drank from his cup again.

"Well, what do you do, when you're about?" she asked, picking up papers from the desk she knew were already in the wrong order and tapping them together.

"Albert Square? It's a joke. 'Excuse me sir, but can you get off the steps, please? The council will be here in a minute and you smell like an arse', or 'Don't feed the birds, they're bastards and they'll just keep coming back.' Honest to God, I'm close to death around there. I'm not a bloody child, I can take a dig or two, why am I on the most boring shift?"

She sat down again in front of him. He had wiped his eyes raw. She put her hands around his. He looked at her with confusion and pleasant surprise.

"Look, I know, it's hard. Yes, you're a street sweeper with handcuffs, we all are. That's the job. But I'll be buggered before you get driven out by an overgrown Bevin boy with a grudge. You're not alone." She smiled at him and his shoulders pulled back, as though relieved of a huge weight.

"I'm sorry for, for that." He gestured behind her.

"No problem. Besides, look around you. Does this look like what I signed up for?"

He chuckled and sat up, forcing a smile through his lips.

"The rest of the station think I'm a joke, don't they?"

"No, they don't, Butterwick. Don't know about me, like."

"At least they call you *Constable*, Sheel."

"Among other things. Would you like another tea? Preferably not thrown?"

He nodded. The condensation from the kettle fanned up the wall like a plume of feathers. She poured into another mug, stained beyond saving, and had her back to him as he spoke again.

"Are you here because of what happened to that paki?"

A drop of boiling water spilled over the side of the mug and scalded her thumb. She clenched it into her fist and held her nerve.

"Well, not in so many words. But you know how the bosses are." She took the tea over to him, handed it over and sat down.

"Come on, Sheel. What do you *really* think? Bit of a waste of time sending the girlies to the primary schools, in't it? What are the sammies getting out of it?"

"Aye, I know. Send 'em back," Sheila uttered, her attention hanging on his response.

"Glad you agree. Absolute savages, have an easier time training dogs."

He drank from his mug and coughed a little as a drop ran down his chin.

"Sorry about that, wrong hole. Was that you the other day?"

"Was what me?"

"The paki in the cells. Was that you?"

"You've already bloody asked me this. I took her in, yeah."

"Are you serious? Love, you know what I mean." He raised his eyebrows, as if they were to drop the penny themselves. Sheila did not move.

"No, I don't. I hope you're not going to take the piss again."

He laughed to himself and took another swig. His eyes narrowed over the rim and the corners of his mouth stretched past the mug at his lips. She felt the condescension like humidity on her brow.

"Out with it then...new boy."

He took the mug away from his face and his smile was gone.

"She did herself in, right?" he said.

"Yes. It all got a bit too much for her."

"It did, did it?"

"Why are you bloody parroting me? I'm trying to be nice, pillock."

"Think about it, though. Did she kill herself?"

"For the last time, yes. All her family died, she was alone, I took her in and cocked up, she hung herself with the blanket I didn't take off her, I'm down here forever. We both know this, the whole blessed division knows this, so what are you getting at?"

"Except she didn't."

"You what?"

"She didn't kill herself, did she?"

Sheila stood up and went to the door. She opened the door and stood next to it.

"Please leave."

"Sheel..."

"You heard. You're a massive piss-taker and I want you to go."

He rose to his feet, knocking his chair back with a petulant kick.

"I know that *you* didn't do it, if that's what you're thinking."

Sheila let go of the door knob, which squeaked to a close.

"Who?"

"Wasn't you, don't know who exactly though."

She leant on the desk, facing him. Sheila knew there was a paper weight within reach. She leant back on her chair in case she had to reach out.

"Oh?"

There was the ghost of a smile on his blank face. She did not want to complete his story for him.

"I wasn't there, but there's talk around the station. Desk Sergeant went for a smoke, quiet night aside from you. He's outside and someone from Women's division went in and, well...did what needed doing."

Sheila resisted the urge to swallow or mop her brow.

"Well. It was going to happen, wasn't it?"

"Sheel, I know that you're a bit soft on people, all the women's division are, fair enough, it's what we need in this day and age. But them lot are coming here, to *our* city, after what *we've* just been through, after all we've *bloody well done* for them, and they're bringing Stone Age barbarism with them." He started to wag his finger as if he was hexing. "They take away jobs, they take away houses, they don't make any effort to speak our language, and now they're killing people, little kids, women, in their beds."

He stopped speaking, not for any dramatic effect, but rather that he had come to the end of a speech that was not his. The words did not sit easy in his mouth and sounded more like an incantation than a raw opinion, as if they were a formality that had to be expressed before they carried on conversing.

"Yeah. Yes."

"Not really meant to tell you this, you know, because the old farts upstairs would see their arse about it. But I'm part of a group. We're getting together to do something about it. Not trying to be bloody nice to them parasites, you know?"

She nodded.

"Look, I'll stop pestering you. But we're meeting tomorrow night. Do you want to come?"

"I would. Thank you."

He stood up and put the cup down on her desk.

"Sorry, again. See you tomorrow!"

He left. For the first time she could remember, she felt glad to be in the quiet. She pulled the drawer open and looked at the hairbrush. There seemed to be more hair than before and she placed the bristles against her nose. With her other hand, she picked up the ice bag, which was full of tepid water, and placed it on her eye. Little feet scraped and scuttled under the shelves.

Sheila felt Rodney make a figure of eight pattern against her ankles as she walked up the garden path, leaving a lime green smear against her legs. Alice stood at the window. She was tapping on the window with her fingernails and half-waving. Sheila opened the door and shoved Rodney out of the way with her right foot. He jumped over the wall into the neighbour's garden.

"Yalright there, Alice love?"

"Oh aye, oh aye, just been pottering. I've got some spuds on the go, some best butter too, do you want any?"

"Yes please, they smell well nice."

Alice glided past her, keeping an eye on Sheila's bruise as she went.

"I tell you, it's getting too dangerous around here. Have you thought about doing something different, Sheila?"

"God almighty, Al, have I ever gone scrapping on the weekend?"

"You may as well, least you can pick your battles there. You wear that uniform and you're a magnet for every cloth-eared git with a shandy in 'em."

Sheila leant against the bannister in the hall as she watched Alice work in the kitchen.

"I fell over. I hit my face. I go to work and get bored to death. I'd rather people swung at me, I'd have a tale to tell."

Alice grunted and lit a cigarette, before she took the potatoes out of the oven. She dished them out on two large, chipped plates and put a fork on each.

"Any sausages?" Sheila asked.

"Do I look like the bloody help?"

"Sor-*ry*. Are you sure you're not telling me owt, Al?"

"No, love, my apologies. I'm like the mad cow in the dress."

"You what?"

"You know, that one who never got married."

"Alice, love, take your time. Just get the words out."

Alice laughed and then grimaced, attempting to summon the memory by force.

"Just, just give me a second. The one in the big house? She was mates with a little boy?"

"Never mind, Alice, I'll just ring up Shady Pines and let them know they need to have room ready, yeah?"

"Oh, never bloody mind, funny bleeder."

Sheila followed Alice into the front room, where they sat and ate. The radio gave more news about troop movements in Malaya and the Clean Air bill receiving a second reading.

"Bit late for Rodney, eh?" Sheila said. Alice said nothing back, munching her potatoes. Sheila finished hers in a few mouthfuls. She stood up and went into the kitchen, rinsing her plate and fork in the sink.

"Don't put it away, love, I'm trying something different," Alice called behind her. She returned to the front room where Alice had stopped eating with half of her plate untouched. She was staring at the radio as the news petered out and the theme to *The Archers* started up. She slumped back on her chair, the plate listing on her knee and the potatoes rolling like ballast. Sheila went upstairs. She went into her room and closed the door.

She sat on her bed and reached under her pillow. She pulled out another one of the returned letters. This one was small and bulky. It took little effort to open. The letter fell onto her lap, folded in haste so it looked more like a star than a letter. She knew its brief message, but she still unfolded it and read.

Dear Marion,

I am so so so sorry about everything.

Please write back. I want to talk to you so badly. I can't stop thinking about you. I might be one for the loony bin if this goes on any longer. Please write me back.

I love you and I love you more,

S.

She shoved the letter back into the envelope. It tore a little at the bottom before she threw it away from her. It sat on the floor, the flap lifted like a prying eye. She looked on the other side of the bed for a magazine. She picked up a copy of Amazing Stories, frayed at the edges and the cover wearing away, and flipped to a page, any page.

Meet the man with no name. Nothing cool about this cat. He was built along the lines of a necktie rack, weighed slightly more than a used napkin, and was as shy as the ante in a crooked poker game.

No sex appeal there, you'd say. Yet within the space of a few days every woman in the country melted into quivering protoplasm at the very thought of this mystery man!

"Oh, *fuck off*," Sheila said, casting the book behind her. She got off the bed and went over to her dresser, where she removed her tunic. She made to hang it on the wardrobe door, when she saw something peek out of her pocket. It was the same peach coloured index card she used in the basement. She took it out and saw scruffy, seismographic writing.

Tomorrow. The Black and Tan, Fallowfield, 8 o'clock. Scrub up a bit. DB.

"And you fuck off, too."

Ten

There was little noise outside of the *The Black and Tan*. Its clientele had dwindled since the war. Its regulars were dying, and other, more vibrant pubs were a short walk away. *The Black and Tan* had a function hall attached, but the pub's policy of no music meant it was used less and less. Yet tonight saw a packed house.

Sheila approached and saw Butterwick outside, pacing and smoking. His hair was plastered smooth, which took his youthfulness to the point of alien. He wore a cheap suit with a skinny blue tie. He saw Sheila approach, wearing a blouse she hadn't washed in a couple of days, and his face lit up. His smile looked as artificial as his hair.

"Sheila, Sheila, welcome, I'm so glad you're here!" He sounded too well-spoken. Sheila nodded and approached, placing a cigarette in her mouth. He scrambled in his pockets and withdrew a zippo lighter, which he thrust at her like a crucifix and flicked five times. It gave a dull, squat blue flame which she had to take two drags on before her cigarette lit. He snapped it closed.

"It's rammed in there. We're excited about tonight's speaker. You know, he's just arrived back from Spain?"

"That's posh," Sheila replied. "Was he on his holidays?"

Butterwick's lip curled up and he affected a laugh.

"No, love, he wasn't on his holidays. He was making contacts for us. Too many reds round here, you see."

Sheila pulled on her cigarette and let him stew in the silence. He was bursting to speak.

"If we're going to take the fight to them, we need friends in other places. Places to hide. You get me?"

Sheila nodded and took another drag.

"There's another thing…"

"Dave?" Butterwick turned to the voice at the door.

"Yeah?"

"Bloody hurry up, it's all starting in a minute." The man disappeared back inside. Like Butterwick, he was in a suit and had sculpted his hair. The pub itself looked near empty through the windows.

"Come on, let's go!" Butterwick took hold of Sheila's arm. She lifted his fingers and pushed his arm back.

"All in good time," she said, "all in good time." He bowed his head, and smiled to hide his disappointment.

Sheila walked in, behind Butterwick, and looked around. People nursed their drinks and stood in the middle of the floor and between tables, not talking, as though they had wandered in by mistake. Butterwick made his way around the barman, who saw him and disappeared into the cellar. They heard sound behind the filthy door at the end of the passage. It scraped against the floor as he pushed it open, and they stepped inside.

A room filled with people, speaking to one another. Voices that made a point of not dropping the letter T or letter H, and stressed words like *immigration* and *commonwealth* to one another. There was a large table, behind which were two flags. An enormous Union jack ran the whole length and width of the wall, and there was a smaller flag above a well-appointed table in the middle. A red background, with a lightning bolt popping across a blue circle in its centre. Sheila swallowed back, even though her mouth was dry. She took a seat next to Butterwick on the edge of the wall seating. A woman on a table opposite caught her eye and smiled, before returning to conversation. Above her, there was a red and black poster with same lightning bolt emblem on it.

Stop Red Violence

Join the Fascist Defence Force

"Have you brought a friend, David?" a blousy voice asked from the table nearest.

"Aye, I have. She's from my work." Butterwick's voice sounded more childish. Sheila looked at the woman he was speaking to. She had thin lips and big eyes under a maroon headscarf.

"I'm Sheila." She reached her hand over, which the woman took with a weak hand.

"Pamela. Do you work with David, then yeah? Is that where you got that?" She waved her finger around Sheila's face, as if Sheila had forgotten it was there.

"Oh, good lord, no. I'm a children's officer..."

"Well, of course, what else would the Jews let a woman do?"

"I'm sorry?"

"Oh, darling, you know what I mean. They won't let you off the leash in a month of Sundays, and you look like you're a real copper, unlike David."

Butterwick bridled a bit and then looked away. Pamela put her hand on his knee.

"Bless you love, but you don't look like a menace to criminals yet. But yeah, *you'll* stay a bitch and then you'll get pregnant and they'll sack you while David does the real policing. But, in our movement, women are up front with the men. We're fighting just as hard against the niggers and the pakis. Jews use them as their stromtroopers and we're meant to shake their hands and just welcome them in, are we? Like hell, we will."

"Yeah, yeah," Sheila nodded. Pamela carried on, railing against the war and the communists as Butterwick nodded. She only stopped when knocking came from the table at the front and the room fell quiet.

"Good evening, ladies and gentlemen. Thank you for taking time out of your lives to attend tonight. I declare this session open." The man, balding and squat necked like a bollard, banged on the table with a fat gavel. The room applauded, although Sheila did not know why. A group of seven men marched on stage with their hands by their sides and wearing the same taking-themselves-seriously expression. Each took a seat, except for one with soft, uneven facial features. His fencing jacket hugged his body which sagged like a laundry bag.

"Friends, neighbours, patriots..." He carried on, for twenty minutes, in the same vein as Pamela. Circular logic, self-conscious language and pompous delivery. Sheila felt herself nodding off, only to be roused by the sporadic applauses, which appeared out of nowhere and lasted for a few manic seconds. She sneaked glimpses over at Butterwick, who nodded, pouted and reclined the whole way through.

"As for our cousins from Asia..." the voice started, before being interrupted by booing. He raised his hand for quiet and carried on.

"They really do think they're clever, don't they? They bring their Neolithic beliefs and disgusting faith to our Christian homeland and then have the nerve to blame *us* for their killing of innocent people. Veterans, shop assistants, even innocent children, all sleeping in their beds and all burned alive! Well I say to them, that if we can live through the *feuersturm* and if Dresden can become German again, then their tribal carnage will not shake us, scare us or conquer us!"

Sheila stirred in her seat as the room clapped again.

"Having said that, keeping them away from us is for the best. If one goat-eating, horse-toothed Sammy wants to set another ablaze, what business is it of mine? But to bring it to our homes, to our neighbourhoods, to our nation, *that*...that is a declaration of war!"

Some of those near the stage stood up as the room erupted again. Sheila looked around and saw a group of people at a table, conspicuous by their lack of clapping.

They wore white, unlike the general black clothing of the audience. There was a gap between them and the other people in attendance. They were wearing neutral expressions, almost appearing gentle. A few wore huge dark glasses which clashed with their white attire. They looked like moths poking through their cocoons. Their attention wandered and they seemed to be looking everywhere, all the time.

"They're a bunch of nutters, them," Pamela whispered.

"Who are they?"

"Tell you in a bit." She turned to face the stage. The speaker was in the middle of his final flourish, which Sheila did not listen to. She was still looking at the people in white. She looked to the back of the room and saw someone she recognised. His head bore a pink scar and his face was lopsided. He also wore large, dark glasses.

Somewhere in the room, *God Save The Queen* started playing and the room came to its feet. Many joined in, dragging the anthem into a funereal dirge. The people in white remained seated. When it finished, their came a cry from the front.

"Seig!"

"*Heil!*" the room responded, right arms raised. Sheila did likewise, looking around at the people in the room. They were too enraptured in their declarations to notice her. The people in white were slow to come to their feet, and they did not engage with the spectacle of salutation. This chant continued three times across the room, before the men on the stage filed off. Some people kept yelling the response while the rest applauded. Another man took the stage and waved the crowd noise down.

"Thank you ladies and gentlemen, please feel free to talk to any of us about how you can get involved and help us out on the ground. We will be meeting the same time next week. Rule Britannia!" He waddled off stage to a brief applause. The room began to talk again. Pamela looked at Butterwick.

"Dave, do us a favour and get us both a gin."

Butterwick rolled his eyes, stood up and walked away. Pamela dragged her chair over and leant on Sheila's table. Pamela waved her closer.

"Don't know their name, but they're big on religion, I think. They come here and just stand around, waiting for people to talk to them. That bloke in the middle were the first. He just hung about for ages and then those women joined him after a bit. They never used to wear those big glasses, they look bloody stupid wearing them indoors." Pamela's eyes were intent on Sheila's handbag as she spoke.

"Want a fag?" Sheila asked.

"Oh, yes please, thanks."

Sheila took her tobacco tin out. A smudged thumbprint on the tin had taken a scrap of paint off the cover girl's chin. Sheila opened the tin and lit both cigarettes before passing one to Pamela.

"How often do you all meet here?"

"As often as possible, big meetings like this once a week but some of us just meet here more often. Landlord doesn't care, we're keeping him in business. Doesn't like yids, either, which helps." She closed her eyes as she took a greedy drag on her borrowed cigarette. Sheila watched her and let her cigarette hang from the corner of her mouth, impatience and boredom rising up within her.

"Is it true what they're saying? That's they're killing people in their beds?" Pamela asked, and then answered her own question. "I know what you'll say, you can't tell me. Dave says that all the time, thought it was just him, but it's probably a copper thing. Can you tell me anything about it? Can you?" Sheila held still for a second and then shook her head slowly. "Well, we've all heard what they get up to. A bunch of us want to get back at them, not sure how yet. Do you see that bloke over there?"

She pointed at the man in the filthy coat. The people sat next to him on the bench had dispersed, leaving him by himself. He stared straight ahead, and his drooling mouth was open.

"Aye, I've seen him around. Village idiot, isn't he?"

"Well, wouldn't say that. He doesn't speak, but he *did* get his brains scrambled by a grenade, so I'm told. Quite a few of them still knocking about round Withington way, apparently."

"Oh aye?"

"Yeah, well, a whole family on his street got it. The mum were the only one who lived, went barmy. Her husband came back from Dunkirk and Crete, only to get burnt alive by a poxy little wog. And your lot seem to be doing bugger all about it."

"Well, we *have* dealt with some Asian families who were victims of arson, too..."

"All the more reason to send 'em home," Pamela snorted. The silence pushed Sheila further away from Pamela like a tide. "Ah, Dave, took your bloody time, didn't you? Thanks."

Butterwick put the drinks down on the table. He sat down and put the glass to his lips. His cheeks rouged around it. Sheila sipped her gin and tonic and nodded at the group in white, who were sitting silent.

"What about them?"

"Oh, he's a fucking loony, him..." Butterwick began. Pamela kicked him in the shin underneath the table and he recoiled.

"Ey, mouth! Ladies present!" She exclaimed, and he looked away. Pamela continued from where her son left off. "Well, they're loons, yes. No idea who that bloke is. He just appeared one meeting and just stared around. See that woman to his left? Angie or Angela or something, she was coming to meeting for a little bit and they started talking. Next thing, she has those big silly glasses on and the two are inseparable. Then that other one, the red head, joins in. Then there's more of them and now there's a bloody squadron of them. They're bloody hard to talk to, too, its like speaking to a brick wall."

She took another luxurious pull on her cigarette, her eyebrows almost interlacing in undue ecstasy. She blew a big cloud into the air, and Butterwick took his chance to speak.

"They call themselves Knights, you know? No one knows where the bloke came from before this. Definitely not from round here, like." He began to clear his throat but saw Pamela about to jump in on his speech, so carried on speaking before he had finished. A trapped bubble in his throat made his voice sound frog-like.

"He started coming to meetings, on and off. Thought he might have been a kike snooping about, you know, but nothing ever happened, so he kept coming and for whatever reason, people keep sitting at his table." He finished what he was saying, nearly out of breath, and returned to his pint. Pamela sipped on her glass as a quiet settled on the group.

"So, what brings you here, love?" Pamela asked over the tip of her tall glass. Her lip stuck out underneath the glass, leaving a smear of lipstick.

"Well, me and... Dave, we started chatting and he invited me down, so I came down."

Pamela swung her look at Butterwick like a cricket bat. He was busy hiding behind his pint.

"Really. What did you chat about? Or was it the kind of chat where *people don't shut their bloody mouths?*" Sheila could hear the italicised words in Pamela's speech.

"No, no, we started chatting, and we were talking about stuff that's happening in town, and he told me about your meetings. I don't want them in town either, they're nothing but trouble, you know, them, the immigrants."

"The *coons*, you mean? The *hajis?* My sister in Canada is an *immigrant*. She works hard, pays her way, unlike these godforsaken leeches coming over here." Pamela shut her eyes and nodded in a manner she thought to be regal.

"I *would* respect them," said Butterwick, "After all, they can scrub a floor pretty well and all that, but England needs to be English, you know? Can't have a nation of toilet cleaners, otherwise everyone'll shit on us."

Pamela tutted.

"How very enlightening, Gandhi - Christ knows how you got out of Malaya," Pamela muttered, "but, yeah, Shelly, sorry, Sheila, where are you from?"

"Well, all over, really. Me mum were from Colne and me dad were from Collyhurst. Had a brother, but he had polio, died when he were ten. I joined right out of school, been in the force for eight years this year."

"Ee, unmarried? Living at home?"

Sheila looked away and then back to the table.

"House got hit."

"Sorry, love."

"It's alright. Not married yet, could say I'm married to me work."

Pamela ran her eyes over Sheila and then she stood up.

"Right, I'm going to the ladies, feel free to chat." Pamela walked into the pub while the chatter continued. Butterwick put his pint down.

"So, how're you finding it?" He possessed the eyes of someone desperate to enjoy themselves, despite everything.

"It's different, aye. That lot, over there, the bloke, your mum said he was big on religion?"

"Something like that. He always talks about *seeing the light* or something else. Proper babble. One thing taking control of the borders, fair enough, but I think he wants a new crusade, the nutty bastard."

"Jews've taken Jerusalem back, bit late innit?"

"Try telling him that, Sheel. I need a piss." He got up and took a couple of steps before he paused, wiped his brow, and continued away. Sheila finished her drink and got up. There were still people in the room talking to one another, but many had left. She made her way across the floor, avoiding men proclaiming and affirming their opinions with one another in a manner that got louder and louder. They had not moved from their table and Sheila was almost stood over them before any of them looked at her.

"Evening. What did you think of tonight?"

The man looked at her and did not blink. He had a look of vacant wonder, as if he was seeing things everyone else was not. The women had small smiles but did not look alive.

"I did not think about it, one way or another."

Sheila shifted her weight to her left foot.

"How come you're wearing white? I thought this kind of thing meant black, you know. Sunday best?"

The man stood up and extended a hand to shake. Sheila reached out and took his hand. His grip was soft, but she felt as if he had a strength he was keeping in check.

"Darkness is our enemy. Light is our way. We must fight the dark. We cannot go back to the dark or let in that which is dark. Do you understand?" His accent was hard to place. He was eloquent yet sibilant, and his vowels landed flat rather than floated. He could have been local, once, until something had changed in him. Or he wasn't local at all.

"I think so, sir."

He smiled and let go of her hand. He tucked his hands underneath his armpits.

"You might, one day."

"Tomorrow, sir?"

He nodded.

"Well, have a good night."

She made to walk away and looked over at the man in the filthy coat. His bald head bore the same horrendous scar and his mouth squirmed over the wreckage of his gums. His eyes hid behind a huge pair of glasses she had only seen on blind men, but she felt his look from behind the lenses. His head tracked her movement as she walked across the room. She turned on her heel and walked over to him. He did not raise his head, and she felt his gaze run through her. His jaw opened and she became aware of a gaping rent under his jaw, through which she could see his breast pocket. It stayed there as he rocked a little from side to side, as if the words did not want to come out of him.

"*Gaar.*"

He slurped his saliva from his lips and looked away. She decided to say it.

"It is the light," she said at the floor, as she turned.

"It is the light," the man and the women replied, in a low congregational tone. The air caught in her throat as an ape-like fist had grabbed her windpipe. Sheila turned and saw them all looking at her. A couple of the women broke out into smiles and the man's eyes filled with tears.

She quickened her pace and entered the pub itself. Butterwick stood at the bar, talking at a man who was drinking. He noticed her and snaped out of what he was saying to the man.

"Sheila, are you going already?"

"Yeah, I've got to go home, I'm on the early tomorrow."

"Well, let me take you home..."

"Butterwick, it's alright. Thank you for inviting me out."

Someone knocked a drink on the bar and caught it, along with a stifled laugh. He looked disheartened, and then asked her, "Would you like to come tomorrow, when you get off shift? Just us two, for a drink?"

"Yes, please."

"Great, see you tomorrow!"

In that moment, he smiled, grasped her hand and kissed it. They stood for a moment. His eyes looked plaintive, but he knew he had made a mistake. She lifted her hand out of his grip and turned to go. She pushed the pub door open and someone exploded into laughter behind her.

"Butterwick? You said your name was Smith, you big twat!"

Eleven

Meredith kicked the table the record player rested on as the record skipped again.

"Bag o' shite. World-Famous-Bury-Market, my arse." He waved off a pair of fruit flies from his segmented apple and put one in his mouth, chewing like a tramp. Sheila sipped her tea from a mug with a hairline crack running across it.

"Think that's just the record, mate. Player looks alright."

"Nah, Sheel, it's fallen off several lorries and then down my stairs." He scraped the needle off the record with a lazy hand.

"Promise not to tell the station what I'm going to tell you?" Sheila said. He scoffed, spraying a couple of apple fragments into the air.

"I bloody knew it, Sheel. No one can just be friends with me, can they?

"Oh, come on, you *are* a friend..."

"You're bloody not, you come here like I'm a sodding human problem page. Don't tell me your secret, love, I saw this coming a mile off." He leant in and exaggerated his features. *"You wear men's underwear, don't you?"*

He giggled as Sheila aimed a slap at him and pouted.

"Swine."

"Aye, course, love. What can I do you for?"

"I went out with Butterwick last night."

He coughed and wiped his mouth.

"Garrett's beanpole? God almighty, you're surely not *that* desperate?"

"Aye, but, it's about that other thing. You know, the girl who died on me?"

He closed his eyes.

"I hope you're not going where I think you are, Sheel."

"No, I don't think it was him..."

"It *was* no one, love. The girl hung herself, for fuck's sake."

"He says different. Says it was someone in Women's that slotted her."

"Did he say who?"

"No, just said it was talk."

"There you go, then. He's a bullshitter, love." He turned to his desk and picked up cigarette, which he lit between two mustard fingers.

"He's a Nazi, too, you know."

"You what?"

"We went to the *Black and Tan*. You know, in Fallowfield?"

"Jesus Christ. Like spending in an evening in a pair of empty bollocks. How'd that work out for you?"

"I'm going back."

Meredith shook his head and smoked.

"What's on your mind, Meredith?"

"Never thought I'd see you become a bootlicker, Sheel."

"I'm not bootlicking!", She cried, "I just want to see if I can get any more titbits. Not from him, but probably from his mates."

"He's got *friends*? Since when?"

Sheila pulled out a cigarette, lit it and crossed her legs.

"Just his fellow imbeciles, you know. I wanted to ask you about one, though. Thought you might have met the geezer during the war."

Meredith sucked so hard on his cigarette the filter squeaked between his lips like a deflating balloon. When he spoke, the smoke, belching out of his mouth, made him seem demonic.

"Sheila, I was a conchie, not a collaborator!"

"No, no, no, Meredith, bloody hell, I mean, as a medic."

He placed the cigarette back into his mouth. Ash fell onto his lap and smouldered for a second before burning out.

"What's he like, then, this man I apparently know?"

"He's in a bad way. I'm convinced he's missing part of his head. The Inspector said that shrapnel made blokes like that. Sound familiar?"

Meredith's cigarette hung from his bottom lip.

"Well, I met a lot of lads who had their brains missing, patients and policemen both." He waggled his eyebrows and picked up his mug.

"Stop pisstaking, Meredith. His jaw's buggered, he smiles like an idiot? And he had a cap in his house, green-rimmed. Sound like any of ours?"

Meredith's eyes widened.

"Irish Guardsman?"

"Is that what the cap is?"

"Aye, yeah. Is he bald? Dribbles?"

Sheila put her tea down and sat forward in her chair.

"Yeah, great big sod-off scar on his head?"

Meredith sat back in half-shock.

"God almighty, I know who you mean. He was a bad bugger, according to the corporal who dropped him off. He was the company badge, you see, professional bastard. Injured on the hills in a *live fire accident*." He flashed his eyes at Sheila before continuing his story. "Took him an age to get better before discharge." He fumbled around on his desk. "Shite, can I rob a cig?"

"Aye, just give me a second."

Sheila pulled out a pair of smokes and passed one to him. He scratched a match along the palm of his hand and perched it between a filthy thumb and forefinger, placing the flame onto his smoke like an aristocrat. He looked up as he inhaled and passed the flame slowly to Sheila, who lit hers. He shook it out with one flick of the wrist.

"Classy, me" he said.

"Like a pigsty", Sheila replied, "Was there anything else? Did he have any visitors?"

"Not from his regiment, they were overjoyed. Sent his medical discharge papers through that week, no one in uniform came to see him after that. But there was a bloke that kept coming to see him. Proper greaseball, wore crap suits, might have been a wop or a spiv or sommat."

"Speak English, Meredith."

"Sorry, your highness. He looked like he'd walked out of a glee club and had slicked back hair when the rest of us stank in week old outfits. Just sat at the man's bedside and whispered to him while the man nodded and smiled. Thought he might have been some religious do-gooder, you know, but he just didn't sit right with me."

Sheila inhaled a lungful of smoke and followed it with a mouthful of tea before exhaling.

"Did you ever chat to him? The suit bloke?"

"No, not that I can remember. He spoke to the patient a lot, though. In his ear. Sun to moon, just whispering in each other's ears. One day, he's gone."

The door opened and Gibbons strode in.

"Morning, Sheila. How's the eye?"

Sheila hesitated.

"Good, now get back downstairs, please."

She left. Sheila stood up and Meredith squeezed his face into a tight gurn.

"Get to work, Sheila, I demand a blood sacrifice!"

"In a bit, loon."

***

The misted windows at the front of the pub did not afford much sunlight. Their patterns were elaborate and twisted around each other like thistle or *fleurs de lis*. A disused mill sat on the other side of the road, which robbed the pub of any of the retreating sunlight. Sheila sat and drank a pint of beer in the corner. The landlord had poured it and then gone straight back to his paper. There was no one else in the pub, it seemed. She wore the same blouse as the night before and her hair was held back by one pin. It was six in the evening. Butterwick would be clocking off in an hour's time.

She drank and tapped her fingers on the table. It was sticky and had several rings from old glasses. Her eyes looked around the room, the ventricle of and old heart ceasing to beat. She looked to her left. There was an old paper back at the end of the bench she sat on. She shuffled up and leant across the bench. She got her fingers on the book and pulled it towards herself. The battered cover obscured its title and it was coming away from its spine, disembowelled of its pages. She cupped it in her hand and turned the pages, desperate to alleviate the boredom.

She flipped over another page. And then another. And another. She could not have cared less for the words. But there were drawings.

On the title, she saw a detailed, nuanced pattern, similar to the one on the chimney breast and the one on the wall at the man's house. The drawing reminded her of the pictures she had seen in her RS books at school. The one where a cross, nothing more than a small piece of wood, shaped like a childish T, was borne to its beholder by a flood of divine light. For the first time, she saw that the circle pattern wasn't one at all. It looked like the sun, but its rays were needle thin and sharp-looking. It could not have been day that was depicted. Whoever had drawn this had shaded in the background. There were clouds, each with their own delicate line work. It shone above a hill. Its rays pierced the ground and each crevasse became visible like a vein. The rest of the book had more and more sketches and outlines and doodles in its margins. They varied in quality, some looking as if they had been added successively, and at speed, by the same hand. Soon after this, towards the end of the book, the writing began.

It is the light.

It is the light.

It is the light.

KOA - away from night

"Hiya, Sheel."

Sheila clamped the book closed and looked up to see Butterwick stood there, still in his tunic, and holding flowers.

"Hiya, Butterwick," she half sang. The landlord snorted back a laugh in the other room. Butterwick leaned in.

"Sheel, for the love of fuck's sake, call me Dave here." He stood back up and looked unsteady.

"Do you want to sit down...Dave?" she sniggered. He pulled the small stool out and planted himself there.

"Got these for you." He thrust the flowers towards her like a lance. She took them and smiled tightly. His nose settled into a near-sneer.

"Are you sure you want to stay in here, Dave? Have I pissed you off?"

"No, excuse me a minute, getting a drink." He stood up again and went to the bar, where the landlord was ready.

"I'm not Dave 'Manly' Smith anymore, my name's Brylcreem Butterwick, the flower-pot man!" he said, his voice high-pitched and airy

"Piss off, Darren!" Butterwick called over his shoulder before disappearing into the men's. Sheila stood up and went to the bar, leaving the flowers behind.

"Hello darling, what can I do you for?" the landlord said.

"Please can I have two golden...sorry, a golden ale and a gin and tonic, please?"

"Course, love." He began pouring and the pump sputtered foam into the glass.

"Ah, damn. Just need to change barrel, bear with us." He lifted the trapdoor in the floor and made his way into the acrid cellar. She could hear him tinkering and then something banged into place.

"Done!" He called out, already halfway up the ladder to the bar.

"Nice cellar, better than the one I work in," she said. He pressed a thin glass up to the wretched gin optic and squeezed out a measure.

"You a copper like Dave, then, yeah?"

"Yeah, I am. Well," Sheila began, making a show of her next words, "*He* goes out and arrests people, I just work in evidence. Spend me days in a basement, like you!"

"Ah, so you do," he responded, "But, pardon me, where did you get that old shiner? Were you roughing up pakis in the cells? Kicking tramps 'cos you were bored?" he carried on, before laughing at himself.

"No, no, no, this is my own stupid fault."

"Well, not to worry. Lesson learned, eh?" He presented the drinks in front of her. She raised an eyebrow and looked at her tepid drink.

"Sorry, sir, but do you have any ice?"

"No."

"How much do I owe you, then?"

"Ee, nothing. If you keep this ne'er-do-well off street corners, then you can have a drink now and again," he stated, nodding over her shoulder as Butterwick returned from the bathroom.

"Darren, have you been pestering the local womanhood again?" Butterwick exclaimed, linking his arm with Sheila's in one quick movement.

"I certainly have not, and she ain't local. Bloody hell, some copper you are!" the landlord bellowed, before laughing again.

"Right, sod off back to your paper and leave me and the lady be," Butterwick said, picking up his beer in one hand while Sheila already had hers. He walked her over to the table.

"Butter...Dave, I'm not an invalid, I know where the table is." She pulled her elbow towards her, but he held on. She sat down, but felt him pushing at her.

"Sheel, please, for the love of God, can't I just have one nice bloody evening? I mean, without you acting like my mum or like that balding twat?" He growled, thumbing at the landlord.

Sheila picked up her drink and stared at him. He seated himself and wiped his hands over his face as if he was cleansing his anger off it.

"Sorry, Sheel. I managed to get out at the last minute, because there was nothing going on, and Garrett doesn't know, so I just want to make the best of it, you know?"

"But there's no need to talk to me like a tuppence-halfpenny tart, is there? Come on, sit down and bloody cheer up. Let's have a drink or ten!" She said, raising her glass. He raised his and they clinked together.

"Course. Not very ladylike, but ho hum," he said, sulking into his glass. She threw the glass back and swallowed the whole thing in one emphatic gulp. He put his pint down.

"Stuff you, and your ladylike, *Dave*." She stood up, taking the paperback with her, and knocked over her empty glass as she got up. She pushed through the doors and into the night. She heard him calling behind her as she made her way up Wilmslow road. His running footsteps caught up with her and he tried to keep up with her, talking as he walked backwards.

"Please, Sheel, I didn't mean it like that, it's been really stressful lately, come on, come back, have a drink with me, don't be like this, put your chin up, yeah? Come and have a drink with me? Alright, I'll walk you home."

He tried to take her arm and she shoved it away.

"Garrett's right, you know. You'd get eaten alive in Territorial, because you're a complete ponce. Now get me a cab or bugger off."

His bottom lip wobbled, and he stormed off, crossing the road and in front of a bus, which honked its horn, and he disappeared into the evening. She walked back to the pub and sat down at the bar. The landlord was rinsing a glass in the sink. No one else seemed to have come in.

"Golden ale, love?"

"Please. Can you put one in the pump too?"

"Course, love."

He pulled the pump, careful and slow, as if it was a surgical art, and then put the pint in front of her.

"Thanks, sir."

"Darren, please. And was that a lover's tiff between you and Mr. *Smith*?"

"God, he wishes," Sheila scoffed, "Is he always like that in here?"

"Well, he acts like an ankle biter, but what else can a young man do in here? Not much fun, us."

"Well, I *am* bored to tears," She said through a grin and drank.

"Ee-arr, that's grounds to get barred, you cheeky cow!" He laughed. She looked to her right into the room where she had sat down with Butterwick. The bunch of flowers had gone.

"Did Butterwick take his flowers with him?"

"I'm sorry, love, I can't get over the fact that he's called bloody Butterwick. He sounds like something off sodding Children's Hour. And no, I gave them away, love." He turned on the tap and ran a pair of glasses under the water.

"Come on, Darren, who'd come in here that'd want flowers?"

"Ask the bloke in the snug."

"What bloke?"

"Well, I'll give you a clue. He looks and talks like a bloke, he's bloke-shaped and he's in the snug. Go and ask him yourself, I want to finish me crossword."

"Alright then, grumpy get. I'll be back for that pint!"

He nodded and leant on the bar over his newspaper. The snug's walls were a deep, rusty green and the furniture was ancient. Two huge chesterfield chairs sat in front of the low roaring fire. She felt as though he was walking into the drawing room of a long-abandoned house. She saw his hand on the armrest and could hear his measured breathing over the sound of the coal cracking and busting on the fire. She approached and sat down in the spare chair. The man from the other night sat there. Like her, his clothes were no different. A white linen suit, which reminded her of a photograph she had once seen of her grandfather, somewhere in West Africa. His shoes had spats on, which she thought looked ridiculous. His sandy hair was combed, but had no product in it. His chestnut eyes rested on her and he smiled.

"Good evening."

"Good evening, sir. I was looking for flowers?"

"They're here." He picked them up from the other side of his chair and passed them over. She held them and looked back at him. He had not moved his gaze. He did not have a menacing face, or at least most men around there pulled when they wanted to intimidate someone. Yet this look was far more searching and arresting than any she had seen, as though he was conducting a telepathic inquiry. She sat back and spoke first.

"How come you took them? Did you forget the wife's birthday, is that why you're here? In the shit at home?" She asked, imploring him to smile the whole time. He paused and then sat up, with his hands on his knees.

"I like beautiful things. I do not like to see them thrown away."

She still could not place him. His accent still sounded flat, but now it also sounded clipped. Nothing about his speech sounded affected, nor did it sound natural.

"Is that an offer? Don't tell me you're bloody married, if you *are* offering."

He tilted his head.

"I already know beauty. I already know bliss. You would not find it in me, but in what I do. In whom I serve." He gestured at the book in her hands. She flipped to the title page.

"What is that?" She asked, pointing and tapping the page. She held on to the book tight with her other hand, expecting him to snatch it off her and throw it into the flames. He examined the page for a moment. He looked at her with delight and surprise, a child desperate to answer teacher's question.

"It is the Light!"

"Yes, it is the light, I know, but can you tell me what the light is?"

His look changed.

"You do not know."

She sat back. He leant towards the fire and stared into it, the flames snatching towards his polished marble eyes. He did not blink. Sweat rolled off his forehead and into his eyebrows as he sat there.

"Sir?"

"All is not all. All is each. Each can be everything to all. Åkeran brings the light to us and banishes the darkness." His eyes met the design again. *Åkeran.* She remembered the inscription on the broken man's mantle. *Aakeran.*

"Right." Sheila took a swig from her pint and pulled another cigarette out of her bag. She leant into the fire to light it and then sat back, taking another mouthful of beer. "So what brings you to Mosley's boys, anyway?"

"I need to be seen. People must come of their own volition. We cannot force people to be with us, it is not our way."

"Some fascist you are, didn't hear Mussolini tell people they had a choice."

"I could not tell you about that."

He wiped his face with his hand and then ran it down his tongue, licking it. Sheila stared and took a long pull on her cigarette.

"We come to banish darkness. Light must be met by more light. We cannot abandon ourselves to night."

"And you do that by burning pakis? Bit of neighbourhood clean-up?"

He did not respond. Sheila took the flowers, held them close to her chest, arose and took a step away.

"Not today. Good night, madam." He stared into the fire. Sheila put the flowers down at the bar and pulled up a stool.

"Those for me, yeah?" Darren said.

"They are if you can give me those ales and a pair of whiskey chasers, mate."

Twelve

Gibbons' sharp knock cut through the basement air. She had no need to knock, as the basement door was already open.

"Kenworthy? Are you here?" she yelled out. She took a couple of steps inside and stopped. Sheila was sat at her desk, her head down, and the ashtray next to her overflowed. Blue smoke settled at eye height in a thin strip like a ruler through the air. Gibbons walked around the desk. When Sheila did not respond, she kicked the rear leg of Sheila's chair. Still, there was no movement. She was conscious - her eyes were open, her back moved up and down with her breathing, her cigarette burned. There was a hairbrush in her other hand, which she pressed against her temple.

"Sheila?" Gibbons shook her by the shoulder. Sheila looked up at her. Her narrow eyes darkened like a wet sand pit and she had crow's feet, great stretching glass-like cracks across her face. These had appeared overnight and were visible despite her dulling bruise. Gibbons perched herself on the desk.

"Sheel. Coming in looking like you've been brawling outside Maine Road is one thing, but answer me honestly now. Are you drinking to excess during the week? Because that's the type of behaviour that travels upstairs far too quickly for me to fix, you know."

"No, Sergeant. I mean, I did have a drink last night, but I didn't get plastered. Had one drink. Ask Butterwick...never mind." She inhaled her cigarette, which had burned down to the filter, and stubbed it out. "That was my last one. I'll have to borrow off Fletch or summat." She rubbed her temples in her hand.

"Don't think you can get one past me, Sheel. I know what hangovers look like. So I'll ask you again..."

"Balls to your hangovers, I'm not hungover." Sheila felt the silence weigh on her. She opened her mouth to apologise, and then didn't.

"You know I don't like being spoken to like that. Once and only once, Sheila. If you aren't hungover, then why this look?" Gibbons bent on her elbow and listened for Sheila's answer. Sheila sat up.

"It's just rough right now. I haven't slept. I feel a bit wrong side out. I can't stop seeing things. I'm not sure how...I mean, it's difficult to...I can't...well, yeah." She reached for her mug and drank the cold, bitter tea, forcing it back before slamming the mug down like a gavel. Gibbons sighed.

"I've seen this before, too. If you need a moment, I can clock you out at three, when the early's done. Again, once and once only, Kenworthy." She had never been this generous, but she sounded sincere. It did not sound like a gift, but a guarded order. Sheila mouthed *yeah* and looked down again. Gibbons got off the desk and went to leave, pulling the door closed behind her. Before it clicked shut, she put her head through the door.

"Don't mention this to anyone or I'll string you up." She closed the door. Sheila put her head on the desk and felt the time pass.

Fletch stood at the entrance, sifting through her bag. Sheila arrived at her side.

"No luck?"

"Nah, Sheel. Left me bloody light somewhere. Pain in the arse, brand new that."

"I'll give you a light if you give me a fag."

"Alright." A few seconds later they were both smoking and walking towards St. Peter's Square. Fletch looked at Sheila as she stared at the ground and took long, regular drags.

"God, you're moody today. Looked better after you got punched, love," Fletch said. Sheila flicked the Vs at her, point blank, and removed the cigarette from her mouth.

"Fletch. I have money, you don't, because you're crap with wages and spend it on looking like Moira Shearer, but after getting kicked in the head by a horse. Don't argue, love. Point is, I need to get steaming pissed and I want you to join me and I'll pay and please can we just go to the fucking pub? Please?"

Fletch laughed behind her cigarette and shot Sheila a look poised between mirth and rage.

"Thank God you're paying or I'd have slapped that fag our your gob. Briton's?"

"Briton's."

They walked the brief distance from St. Peter's Square to The Briton's Protection. It had just opened its doors. They had a window of a few hours to drink without having the bother of other officers. Sheila entered first and they walked past the main bar and towards the back.

"I'm going to park myself. G and T, love." Fletch disappeared into the back room. Sheila stood at the rear of the bar and waited to be served by a paunchy, middle-aged man, who was cursing a large bottle of gin he was trying to wrench off the optic stand.

"Give us a second, love, won't be a mo." He pulled again and something snapped. He dropped the bottle and it bounced once before cracking on the floor. "Oh, sod it. What can I get you, love, before I lose me rag?"

"G and T, pair of house whiskeys and a golden ale, please. And ten fags and matches."

"Aye. Go in the back, I'll bring it round, love, I'm up to me neck in it here."

Sheila walked into the back and saw Fletch touching at her hair in a small pocket mirror. The room smelt of furniture polish and the fire was small.

"You leave the drinks at the bar then, yeah? Making my life difficult?"

"He's bringing them round, calm yourself." Sheila sat down opposite her. Fletch snapped her mirror closed and put it away. She balanced her chin on top of folded hands in a girlish pose and began to soften her words against her teeth.

"So, I'm into knitting, flower arranging and being treated like a moron by big ugly bleeders who work in the hat factory," she began, fluttering her eyes, "as long as they've got one on them!" She pulled her truncheon out and placed it on her skirts, facing skyward. Sheila rolled her eyes.

"You're anyone's for a bag of chips, you."

"Tell that to your fellow Gillettes, Sheel. Ee-arr, is he bringing them through or what?"

The man appeared as Fletch finished her words. He brought the glasses through and put them on the table like he was handling explosives.

"I'll bring your fags in in a sec." He stood up, mopped his brow and went out of the room.

"Did you buy these, Sheel?" Fletcher asked, holding the ochre whiskey up.

"Aye. I'm serious, I want to be flat-on-my-arse drunk." Sheila picked up her glass, clinked it against Fletcher's and threw it back. It tasted like a glass of stomach acid, and Sheila already took a swig of beer to fight back any reflux. Fletcher shuddered and sipped her gin.

"Lord almighty, you're not joking."

"No. Shit show. Whole thing's been a shit show lately. Just want to get ratted."

Fletcher produced a pair of cigarettes and passed one over to Sheila. The man arrived around the corner and decanted more cigarettes on the table, along with a small box of matches. Sheila opened the box and lit a match. They both leant in and ignited their cigarettes like sentries, like lovers. Sheila took another drag, and another, before exhaling a large, thick cloud over the table.

They continued drinking for the rest of the afternoon and into the evening. At first, their orders were consistent - golden ale, whiskey, gin and tonic - but soon they tried anything, and they continued to slip deeper and deeper into the drink. The main bar rocked with clamorous laughter as night fell. A couple of people sat at different tables in the room. Fletcher threw back another whiskey and propped herself up on the table.

"So. Why're you boozing, Sheel?"

Sheila lit another cigarette and dropped the match onto the seat next to her. She slapped at the match, which was already extinguished when it hit the bench, until it flew off and she was sure there was no fire.

"Well, Fletch, Fletcher, my mate, why shouldn't I be?" Sheila's voice was thick, wax-coated and heavy. Fletcher sniggered like a panting dog and smiled as an afterthought. Sheila grinned too, quaffing another mouthful of beer and smacking her lips.

"No, no, yeah, I know, but like, why are you getting plastered now? Did Gibbo say no to your proposal?"

"Cheeky get. Nah, nothing like that. Just like. Well. Its hard. Like, everything's hard." Sheila swigged her beer and part of it ran up her cheek and out of her glass. It dripped onto her chin and ran down her neck. She sat with the beer in her mouth, swelling her cheeks, and then forced it back. Fletcher drank the rest of her gin and tried to look at Sheila.

"I mean, is the job getting a bit much?"

"Aye. Losing me mind a bit."

Fletcher played with her empty glass for second.

"You never gave two shits before, love, why now?"

Sheila turned her pint glass upside down on the table. Suds from her ale dripped on the table and ran up to the rim of the glass like worms in a bell jar. She placed her chin on the glass and looked at Fletcher through half-open eyes.

"You know, like, you must know, those lads who went somewhere with the army and then they'd come back and they'd be punching their mums and kicking puppies and scrapping with everyone?"

"Me uncle Phil was like that," Fletcher said, dangling her finger, "he went to fight the nips and came back a bastard."

"Yeah? What did he say...did he tell you...what...how was he a bastard?" Sheila's head slipped off the glass, which fell on its side. She wheezed out a laugh.

"Sheel, you're such a bloody lightweight, you. He was just nasty, you know? Called me a whoring see-you-next-Tuesday, the bastard, and I was only fourteen! Drank dark rum with his brekkie and tried squaring up on me dad once."

"Bloody hell. How'd that end up?"

"He were pissed, me dad knocked him on his arse. Wasn't too hard, you know how they are." Fletcher sniffed at the whiskey and winced, as she had done the last few mouthfuls.

"I'll have it, Fletch, if you don't want it."

"No, it's alright. I'm already skedging it off you, I'll drink it."

Sheila snatched at the glass, but Fletcher drank it and put the glass down in one quick move, smiling through her clear discomfort.

"Fuck's sake."

"What's the matter with you today, Sheel? Mouth like a sailor, you wouldn't say boo to a goose usually. You been on street corners? Going out with great big hairy-marys?"

Sheila palmed and shoved a cigarette into her mouth and struggled with her strike-anywhere match.

"Well. You won't believe it, but I went out with Butterwick yesterday."

Fletcher's jaw dropped and her eyes widened.

"No? That sack of wet cabbage?"

"The very same, love." Sheila tried to smile, but only bared her teeth.

"God almighty, you need help, woman."

"Think you're right. Binned him off, he's useless, he is." Sheila saw a man in a white shirt move across the doorway and flinched. She thought of the cluster of people at the meeting. She thought of the Keeper and his non-expression by the fire.

"Sheel?"

"Fletch. I have to tell you summat."

Fletcher refocused her eyes as Sheila sat up.

"Let's finish these and go on the canal for a bit. I want to sit somewhere quiet." Sheila pulled her bag towards her as if she was wrangling and animal. Fletcher put two unlit cigarettes into her mouth and stood up.

"It'll smell like a tramp's arse round there right now. You feeling alright?"

"Yeah." Sheila edged out from behind the table and stumbled for a couple of steps, regaining the agency in her legs. They snaked through the pub and out into the street.

Thirteen

They took sideways steps down the canal bank to the brick and gravel path below. The water had a pleasant ripple in it and the moon sparkled off its reflection. Sheila hit the bank and put her hand up for Fletcher to grab.

"I'm alright, Sheel, I'm alright. Let me just-" Fletcher fell forwards, and windmilled her arms as her legs kicked out, trying to find any surface. It looked at if she ran down the bank and into the small rail next to the water.

"M'alright, Theel, M'alright!" Sheila parrotted, tongue fat and deep voice. She let out a filthy, snorting set of giggles. Fletcher steadied herself and flicked the Vs. Sheila sat down on the bank, crossing her legs as she went as if she was folding herself up.

"Come on, Fletch. Sit here." She patted the wet ground and Fletcher came over. A flat-bed truck rattled on the bridge above them and honked its horn.

"Sheel, you're bladdered, and your skirt'll be covered in shite."

"Don't care, just come here. Sit down here."

"I'll crouch, then, how's that?"

Fletcher bent down. Sheila knocked her back with a little prod which threw her off balance and she landed on her backside. Sheila started laughing and pointing. Fletcher sat up.

"I'll have your guts for garters, Sheel, you complete moo!"

Sheila kept laughing and it spread to Fletcher like a pleasant scent, making her smile to herself. She sat up, covered in grit and pale mud, and let Sheila calm herself down before she spoke.

"Sheel, this is a bit out of the ordinary, but why-"

"We're sat where she was, you know?"

"You what?"

"Give us a light and I'll tell you." Sheila seemed to have produced the cigarette from nowhere. She was too drunk to be subtle with her bag. Fletcher dug into her tunic pocket and gave her the nearly half used book of matches. Sheila ran one across her shoe sole and lit the smoke. She exhaled. Her demeanour had changed and there was something composed and lethal in her face.

"So. Who was this she?"

"A bit ago, this. Before your time. I did my probation on Gibbo's beat and she thought I had a big gob. So, when I passed out, she put me in the basement. Worked with a girl down there. She were the only reason I didn't leave, you know. Leggy, blonde hair, great big hundred watt smile. Loved it with her. Loved her, full stop."

"Hang on, *leggy*? You sound like a bloody tomboy...wait, are you?"

Sheila half-laughed and half-choked on her cigarette.

"Why's that a surprise, love? You were making dyke jokes with the rest of 'em."

Fletcher's face struggled to uncross itself.

"Aye, but I just thought that were just boys being boys, you know? Saying you batted for the other team because you gave them stick, I were doing the same."

Sheila pulled on the cigarette and lay back onto the wet earth, her damp hair matting together like antennae.

"Well, I am a tomboy. Marion, her name were. She were only young, 18, fresh out of school. Would have never guessed it but we were peas in a pod, us two. She liked all that space crap and dirty jokes and smoked like hundred a minute. She laughed like a jackal, she did. I was half tempted to never let her stop laughing. She lit up when she laughed, and I lit up with her. Absolute golden girl, she were."

"If you're gonna say that you did the dirty on this spot, then you can piss off, its grim."

"What, and you having it away with Wolfe in his office ain't? Anyway, do you want to hear me story or not?"

Fletcher thought about summoning some rage, but the alcohol made it hard for her to do this and also get up at the same time. She slipped on her hand and ended up sat down again. She nodded at Sheila to continue.

"We met up at the Imperial one night. I doubt the people that made *X: The Unknown* thought that me and Marion would be the ones with their arms round each other, but there we were!" Her final words rang off the bridge walls and the canal seemed quieter for a moment. "We jumped into each other's arms when that bloke got barbecued, and I snatched a kiss off her. Thought that I'd overstepped it and went to go when the lights came up, but she kept me there. When the room were quiet, god almighty, you would have thought kissing made you rich!"

"Aye, it can, down London Road, Sheel. Can introduce you to a few pros, if you want?"

Sheila aimed a gentle slap at Fletcher's leg.

"Cheek. Anyway, me landlady liked me 'friend' coming over and didn't bother us, so we made a little nest in there.."

"Spare me the details, its filth, utter filth!"

"Shut it, Fletch! We had an outstanding practice in that bloody basement, all the packages were in order, in the highest traditions of the constu…constabler…force. No mould, no dust, uniforms pressed, and every courtesy shown to any dickhead, hungover DC or mouthy porter we had to be nice to. And we were properly in love, you know? Like, really in love. Flowers and pressies type of thing." She flicked away her cigarette. Fletcher noticed a tear running down Sheila's temple.

"Sheel?"

"Aye?"

"You alright there, love?"

Sheila twisted her mouth.

"One day, she told someone upstairs, not sure who, didn't matter once she blabbed. Told them about us and then everyone bloody knew. Jesus nutters left bibles on me desk when I weren't there, got my arse pinched about eight times a day and then, top it all off, some daddy's boy cadet tried snogging me on the corridor. Didn't announce himself, nothing. Just arrived and waved his tongue at me like a shit bloody dragon."

Fletcher produced another pair of cigarettes, lit them both and passed one to Sheila.

"What did you do?"

"Slapped him and he bit his tongue. Blood everywhere, like this." Sheila writhed on the floor making gargling noises and crossing her eyes.

"Then what?"

"Oh aye, oh aye, don't whinge, just telling me tale." She played with the cigarette in her fingers for a moment. "I get dragged into Wolfe's office by Gibbo, he gave me a bollocking. 'Blah blah don't slap new boys' etcetera, etcetera. Got sent home. Tried to keep myself from taking it out on Marion, but just had enough that day and told her to pack up and fuck off. She did." Sheila smoked and kicked her heel against the floor.

"Is that it?" Fletcher said, scratching behind her ear. "I'm covered in crap, I'm cold and need a wee, hurry up."

"Right, right, right, one day she shows up dressed like a London Road pro and all the lads are whistling at her and calling out to her and being right arseholes, I ask her why and she says she's with CID and I should mind my own business. So I did. And it was the biggest mistake I've ever bloody made." Sheila dropped cigarette ash on her face and she swatted it off, her story taking over her. "They were sending her down here, you know? Some horrible bastard had been attacking women down here and that's why they sent her, probably. Should count myself lucky, in that case. They only pinched my arse, they sent her down here, the fuckers. On her own. At night. No partner, no baton, not a sodding whistle, just expected the rest of CID to be in the right place at the right time and they bloody weren't and here, Fletch, *right fucking here*, where *I'm lying right now*, he bashed her head against the railing I'm next to and carried on bashing her when she were on the ground, face down in a puddle, knocked out, and he were at her knickers when they got him!" Her breath was sharp and stuttering. Her eyes were wild. She carried on, the words taking a life of their own as she struggled to hold onto them.

"Got her an ambulance just in time, they said, and not a single one of them arseholes went to check on her in the hospital, not one, I found out the day after and had to go on me lunch and, Jesus Christ almighty..." She sobbed and the bridge's echoes gave each one a grim weight. "They had her in one of those massive breathing machines, said that she would've died if she they'd got to her a second later. The only thing I could see were her head, like it'd been cut off. Me brother died in one of them - polio. I just couldn't handle her going the same way. So I left her there. I left her there on her own. I didn't leave the basement for a month after that and then, when I'm about ready to see her again, bloody Gibbo comes down and tells me she's gone to Lancashire and I'll never see her again. " Her crying made each drag she took long and shallow. Fletcher edged over and put her hand on Sheila's arm.

"Did she?"

"Don't know. Keep writing her letters but I've never got one back."

Fletcher rubbed Sheila shoulder, as if she were rocking her. Sheila continued to cry, her cigarette extinguished by a puddle at her side.

"I'm a terrible person, Fletch."

"Oh, shut up, Sheel, have you ever robbed anyone? Or shot or stabbed anyone? Plenty of our bods have, you know..."

"No, love, but people have died 'cos of me. I'm sick of being around and feeling powerless to do fuck all when there is definitely sommat sinister going on and no fucker believes me."

Fletcher got to her feet and grabbed the handrail.

"God's teeth, not this again..."

"You know Butterwick?"

"And this, too! What about him, he's a scrote, so what?"

"You know how I went out with him, yeah?"

"Aye?"

"He said someone knocked the paki in the cells and that he said he knew it was a woman."

Sheila turned her head and looked at Fletcher, who stood over her and keeping a foot within stamping range.

"I hope you're just drunk."

"Well, Fletch? Do you know owt?"

"You're one to talk, you gave her blankets and didn't take them away."

"Aye, true. I know it weren't you, you were probably upstairs with Wolfe, talking with your mouth full, yeah?"

Fletch kicked her in the shoulder and leant against the railing, dangling her head in the breeze above the water.

"So what's your point? I'm bored shitless here."

"He got me thinking that maybe he knew who did it. He invited me to a meeting with his *friends*.

"Fuck off, he's got mates?"

"Met his mum and all sorts."

"No you bloody didn't, Sheel! Really? He's such a bloody bedwetter."

"He's a blackshirt too, you know."

"Well, doesn't surprise me. Weren't a day that went by where he weren't making snide remarks."

"No, Fletch, but like, really, he does *heil hitler* and all that. That's where he took me."

Fletch sat down again, the puddle splashing behind her as she hit the ground.

"That's awful. I mean, come on, I've had some difficult times in me life and some rubbish nights out, but never with a bloody goose-stepper. Jesus, doing the slosh is bad enough."

Sheila hawked and spat to her right before wiping her mouth.

"It wasn't the weird bit. I met this bloke who was in white. Him and a bunch of women. They all said *it is the light* to me. Like loads of people at the house burnings. So I went back the day after and met the bloke again."

"Oh aye? Anyone we'd know?"

"A bloke we'd pegged as a dead end was with him, you know the one I got brews from?"

Fletcher lay back, the drink slowing them both down.

"Oh aye, the one who was a bit slow. Hang on, you'd only know that if you had my notebook, which went missing?"

"Aye, I nabbed it, sorry."

"Slippery bitch, you. Give it me back!"

"I will, in a bit. But yeah. They're the ones doing the burnings. They like super weird, don't think they're Christians. Lots of browns and blacks in their ranks."

"Some blackshirt, then."

"Well, he were wearing white."

Fletcher rubbed her head in her hands.

"I'm too bloody drunk for this right now. Can we go home?"

Sheila did not reply.

"Sheel? Can we do one?"

A fat, cavernous snore was Sheila's response. One eye

closed and the other showing half an eye, alcohol having

switched her off. Fletcher sighed and walked into the dark

under the bridge. She hitched up her skirts and started peeing,

keeping any eye out for anyone prowling along the desolate

bank. She noticed a pair of figures in white, in the distance as

she was finishing. She stood up, straightening herself out, and

stared at them. She walked over to Sheila, keeping her eye on

them on her way. She pulled Sheila up by her shoulders and

pushed her back up, the wet silt up her back like old crumbs.

She pulled her to her feet, where Sheila stood, half awake.

Fletcher looked back over her shoulder and the two figures

were gone.

The smog rolled through the streets as Fletcher propped Sheila up by her underarm and pulled her down the street, their feet kicking through dead leaves as they went. Sheila dug her heel into a tree root which burst through the pavement. She took hold of the tree and pulled away from Fletch, who tried to pull her back. Sheila held on and managed to tear her other hand away, clasping both around the trunk. Sheila slid down it to her knees, scraping her hands, wretched and was then sick. It pooled around her knees, soaking her tights and dripping down to the gutter.

"God's sake, Sheel. My mum's going to royally kick off, get up."

Fletcher got Sheila to her feet like a fawn. They made their crooked way up the street until Fletcher fished her keys out with her one free hand and opened the door. Sheila tripped on the front step and fell on her face, knocking Fletcher over. The wooden floor clattered under their bodies. The pair of them started laughing like foxes as they tried to get up. The upstairs landing light came on.

"Abigail, what in God's name are you doing pratting about at this time?"

"Oh, shurrup, mum, we've just been for a drink."

"We! I'll knock your block off if you've brought a bloody lad back here..."

Her mother's feet banged against the stairs as she ran down. She gripped the bannister as she saw them both writhing drunk.

"Oh my holy God in heaven, what do you think you two're going as?"

"Mum, for fuck's sake..."

"Don't you bloody well use that language with me!"

"Mum, mum, mum, relax, just go back to bed."

Sheila was trying and failing to roll on her back. She cackled at the exchange on the stairs.

"I'll be seeing *you* in the morning, Abigail."

She went back upstairs and slammed the bedroom door.

"Sorry about that, Sheel, she's a right cow," Fletcher slurred.

Sheila tried to respond but could only manage an interrupted groan.

"Right, you need to go sleep, love. Let me sort you out."

Fletcher got up and shut the front door. She got Sheila onto her knees and led her into the front room. There were a group of chairs around a table with a wireless in the corner. Fletcher let go of Sheila and pulled a bunch of tartan-patterned blankets off a chair behind her and tossed them on the floor next to Sheila, who pulled an edge towards her and placed it under her head.

"Don't go to sleep yet, love, just give me a minute."

Sheila swilled the water around her mouth and spat it into the bowl Fletcher offered. Her clothes had cleaned up easily with a wet cloth and now lay draped over chairs and over the mantelpiece. She sat, unsteady and swaying, as Fletcher got rid of that night's stains.

"Thanks again, love, you didn't need to do all of this, love."

"Bollocks, Sheel, you look like a very drunk person. Come on, have another swill, I can smell your breath from here."

Fletcher put the glass to Sheila's lips, and she swilled and spat again. She bared her teeth to Fletcher and started laughing and snorting.

"Right, bed now, you lunatic, we're on the early."

She stood up to take another blanket and she felt Sheila clutch her ankle.

"Oi, hands off, you silly mare," she laughed. Sheila pulled herself up and grabbed her thigh with her other hand like a ladder.

"Sheila, for God's sake, let me get...Sheila!"

Sheila pulled her by the back of her knee to the floor next to her and held her tight.

"Do you want to go to sleep tonight..."

Sheila planted a kiss onto Fletcher. They were still for a moment. Sheila relented to take a breath and went to kiss her again. Fletcher wrenched herself away and got to her feet.

"Here's your blanket, goodnight."

She chucked the other blanket towards Sheila, who caught it on her outstretched arms.

"Oh love, look, I'm sorry, I don't know what…"

Fletcher was out and closed the living room door behind her. Sheila sat back in the dark and pulled a cushion off a chair behind her for a pillow. The room span and chugged away at her vision, refusing to align or stay still. She closed her eyes.

Fourteen

Children's footsteps sang off the pavement and cobble stones as grey morning light pierced through the curtains. Sheila pushed herself upright, only to fall back with a puncturing headache. A metallic glare smothered her vision. She rolled onto her front, desperate for the ballast in her head to right itself. Her tunic spread over the sofa like a stain. She crawled towards it, feeling alcohol and bile slush against her stomach, and shook as she held back a wretch. Her tongue felt like old suede against the roof of her mouth. She grabbed one shoe by the buckle and pulled it over. When it was halfway on, she realised was still wearing her tights, but nothing else. She got up and looked around the room. Her knickers were in front of the fireplace. She grabbed them and half hopped and wrestled herself into them. She picked up her vest and her thumb ran squashed a globule of vomit. She dropped it and went for her blouse, and then her skirts.

Someone cleared their throat in the doorway next to her. Her arms burst across her body and she retreated, her hangover upsetting her balance. An older woman, a walking caricature in pinny and hair curlers, entered the room and folded her arms.

"Well, I'm going to be having words with my Abigail later. You utter, utter disgrace. To think that people like *you* are allowed to police *us* nowadays..." She carried on. Sheila felt her body set the hangover back, doing her a favour while she gathered her clothes. She knew she was late, but now that Fletcher's mum was scolding her, she took her time getting ready. She recalled the way she felt in school, as Sister Mary Francis popped her ear drum upon finding her and a classmate *rehearsing in the chapel.* She replaced each button on her blouse like steps on the slow march, and each item of clothing became an event. Fletcher's mum did not calm down but stopped yelling after a while and just stared at her. Sheila replaced her cap and picked up her bag, which still had its contents, before brushing past Fletcher's mum's shoulder and out of the house. Her hangover regained its ferocity as she made her way up the street and, hog-tied by the sickness, she turned into a ginnel and vomited. She pulled her stained vest out of her bag, wiped her mouth and stuffed it back before she carried on up the road, emerging at Palatine Road.

The bus journey felt bumpier than usual. Everything felt slower on the road. Pressing through Fallowfield and Rusholme, the city seemed busier than usual through the light rain sheet. She pressed her head against the window as the bus moved, rolling the coolness across her head as they went. She mouthed her explanation to herself, eyes closed and prayer-like.

I've been feeling a bit poorly lately. I'm sorry I'm late, I'll have to see the medic at some point. I'll make up the hours in overtime. I promise...

Anderson Street's steps were quiet, to her relief. She moved as fast as she could, each step strategic, and her hangover stayed dormant, a madman sitting in the doorway of his open cage. There was no one in the foyer and the desk sergeant was busy berating an underling in the office behind his desk. She moved past him and towards the basement. She fitted her cap on her head, gearing herself up for a fight, as she made her way downstairs. The door to the basement was closed. She took a breath and pushed it open.

No one was at the desk, and fresh butts joined her overflowing ashtray on its sides. She dropped her bag on the floor and started to pace down the long walls of shelving.

"I'm here. If you're here to give a bollocking or take the piss, come out now and speak your piece, otherwise piss off so I can die in silence." Her words met no reply, the lights flickering and the pipes tapping above her. She walked into the darkened end of the shelves and forced her way through a gap in the shelves. There was something underfoot.

A rat's corpse had mingled with soaked, composted cardboard, making the whole stretch of floor resemble dead flesh. She dragged her foot across the floor as she made her way up the corridor, hearing something grind against the floor beneath her. The gravelly noise did not go away, no matter how hard she scraped, and the smell became more intense. Her desk was in sight and she felt desperate for a smoke, if only to take the stench away. She retrieved her bag from the floor, holding her breath as she got down to pick it up. She pulled the tobacco tin out, now with no woman left on the cover, and pulled out a pair of cigarettes. One strike anywhere match remained out of the book she had from the previous night. She ran it across the desk where it lit, and she smoked both cigarettes. She crossed her legs and saw what was attached to her shoe.

Wet, dirty, but unmistakable, like diamonds amid clods of dry earth. Threads of white gold hair, impervious and untainted by the dirt. She pinched one end from her heel and pulled. It did not stop, and she pulled at the heel again. Something stirred across her shin. She pulled again and felt the same sensation across her thigh, and begin to stir on her groin, where it stayed, teetering and dancing, until her pore stopped it with a pinch. She yanked the golden hair, expecting it to pop out. It did not. She tried again, and it no longer felt like hair. It felt like steel wire, or rope, that had fixed itself around her pelvis, and could not be budged. She took it in both hands and pulled up like a theatre hand. The incisive, wincing pain burned through her lower stomach, into her spine and across her shoulders. The burst came. She yelped and she pulled the hair through her hands. The pain trailed off with the hair. As the final stretch came across her hand, it left a snake's trail of blood across her palm.

"Sheila?"

She jumped back and looked at the door. Gibbons entered and went around Sheila, meeting her eyes as she went, as if she was intruding.

"Sarge?"

"I won't be a moment, Sheel. Do you have a smoke?"

Sheila blinked a couple of times and mouthed a response, before managing, "What?"

"Sheel, do you have a fag I could rob?"

"Err, yes, yes I do, Sergeant." Sheila pulled out another cigarette for Gibbons, who was sorting through the papers on display, confused and frantic. Sheila had never seen her in this state. She held the cigarette out in front of her like an exclamation point. Gibbons took it and sat down on the instant. Gibbons was no smoker. She sucked like a child with a sundae, finger and thumb pinching in an A-OK manner, eyes wide and cheeks concaved. A spitting exhale followed every drawn-out inhale. Sheila had to look away and laugh to herself a couple of times at Gibbons' display.

"Is everything alright, Sergeant?"

Gibbons dropped her half finished cigarette and stamped it against the stone floor. She stayed still for a moment and then took Sheila's hands in hers.

"Sarge, is everything…"

"Bloody no. It's a disaster, and I am shocked and appalled to my core if what I hear is true."

"If this is about me getting drunk after you told me to go home…"

"Sheel, I wish. I really bloody wish. There's a lot of talk upstairs. The senior officers have been screaming their heads off all morning and they've screamed at me in turn. But you need to tell me the truth, right now. Please."

"Yes, Sergeant."

Sheila felt cold.

"Are you a Blackshirt? And don't lie, or I'll know."

"No, Sergeant. Absolutely not."

Gibbons let go and stood up.

"Wolfe wants to see you upstairs, now. Bring your bag."

Sheila's backbone seemed to evaporate and her shoulders hit the table lip behind her as Gibbons went to go. She put her hand on Sheila's shoulder and squeezed.

"I was always very fond you, Kenworthy." She walked out, her head slumped against her chest as she went. She sniffed as she left the room.

Sheila's way up to CID was as quiet as her entrance. The detectives were subdued from their usual noise and bravado. She walked across the room to the corner office. A hush descended on the room as ears tuned in to what was to come next. She knocked.

"Enter, Kenworthy."

She walked in and closed the door behind her.

"Please sit."

"No thank you, sir." She stretched her legs by tensing her calves. There was a creak on the floorboards behind her. She looked over and the Inspector stepped out of the darkness.

"Sit down, constable."

She did as he said. Wolfe drained his mug and belched.

"Its come to my attention that you're not happy with being booted out of the investigation and, instead of taking this on the chin like any other good copper, you've stuck your nose into business you had precisely no reason to be involved with. Is this right so far, Kenworthy?"

"If you say so, sir."

He slammed his palm against the table and shot to his feet.

"Don't bloody well treat me like some half-arsed, chip-shop commander, Constable!" He roared. She jumped back at the noise. He perched himself on the desk by his fists.

"Do you think we're as stupid as you are, woman? That a day book from CID would just *vanish*? It reappeared on our desks today, it may interest you to know. One phone call to Wythenshawe confirmed your presence there, and then you *must* have gone to the house afterwards. Fell over and got a black eye, did you *fuck*! A few days after this, you're seen leaving a meeting of Mosleyites and, according to what we've heard, you've openly conspired with the people claiming responsibility for the arsons. Blackshirt murderers! Not like me and your Inspector and half the *sodding* station saw their mates killed so we'd never see their ilk again, let alone have one in uniform! I have only one question, really. Beyond fascism, insanity and murder, what in all of God's creation possessed you? What the hell is wrong with you?"

Sheila was stunned. She felt as if she had been shot in the throat.

"Here's what happens next. Go home. A courier will retrieve your tunic and give you your final take home wage later this week. You're a wolf with no teeth, Sheila, and a disgrace to the uniform. Get out of my office and get out of my sight."

Sheila stood and saluted. The Inspector caught her hand from behind and pushed her arm back down to her side.

"You're not a copper any more, stop pretending to be one," he said, his voice scraping against his throat. She stepped back out of the office and left the door open, reeling through the room. Having spent her whole working life avoiding their faces, their smiles, their utterances, she now found there were none. Eyes honed in on piles of paper. Mouths which never closed retreated under a moustache or fixed themselves in a line. She felt as if she was stumbling through a room of mannequins. She reached the door and grasped it by its hinges, staving off a faint. Heels stomped up the wooden staircase, and whistled a worker's tune. Sheila looked down and saw Fletcher emerge into view, carrying documents and smiling from ear to ear. The smile disappeared as their eyes met.

"Y'alright, love? You look a bit peepy from last night."

Sheila took the two steps down and pushed Fletcher, who flung the documents into the air. Sheila got one look at her face as she passed her tipping point, and regretted what she had done. Fletcher rolled down the stairs, hitting step after step, a delicate cog pounded into nothing by a relentless machine. Her face met the wall below and a noise between a crack and a clap sounded, before she slumped over. She did not move, a pile of clothes worn by a pile of bones. Sheila grasped the bannister, holding herself upright as her legs threatened to give way. Two men flew past her down the stairs and dropped to Fletcher's level to tend to her. Another arm grabbed her under her arm and frog-marched her down the stairs and through the station. She did not care to look at who marched her away and, by the time they reached the front door, the person was dragging her. They went through the door into the rain at a disheartening speed and she closed her eyes, preparing to be thrown down the front steps. All of a sudden, the movement stopped and the hand let go. The person walked away into the station behind her. She turned around and saw Butterwick standing at the front desk. DCI

Wolfe stepped into view and shook his hand. Cahill appeared, chucked her bag out of the door and closed it in her face.

She careened back onto Oxford Road, lurching towards her bus stop. Her only relief was that it was the middle of the day and the streets were not bustling with pedestrians. A bus pulled up and she got on, falling onto the nearest chair as it jump-started down the road. She dug around in her bag and pulled out the tobacco tin. There was one cigarette left and she had no matches left. She bit harder and started to chew. Tobacco flakes ran around her mouth like lice and the paper stuck itself in her teeth and onto her gums. She started to cough as part of it caught in her throat.

A sickly heat spread across her face and she knew she had to get off the bus. A freight train clattered across the bridge at Oxford Road station overhead. She pulled herself up and swung from bar to bar. Her sodden brow ran over her eyes and the street began to split into two. Walkers, vehicles, lamp posts, buildings all multiplying like amoeba in a Petri dish. Her hand missed a bar and she spun round. Her head bounced off the floor and she lay there. She vomited again, an orange ooze which ran across her tunic. The bus halted, sending people forward in their seats as if they all nodded in agreement. She felt a rough hand pinch her arm as it pulled her to her feet and ushered her off onto the street. He was swearing the whole way, and she recognised he was speaking, but the words sounded alien. A series of infuriated sounds and emissions which lost all sense to her ears. She staggered and hit the back of the bus shelter before she turned around to see the driver get back on the bus and pulling away. The people around her appeared unmoved and kept on looking at the floor, or the other side of the street, or into shop windows, or at the paper. No one spoke a word.

Fifteen

Darren placed the glass in front of Sheila's head as she rested it, face down, on the bar top.

"Are you sure you're in a fit state, love?"

"Yes," she said, muffled by the bar, "Just waiting on a friend."

He started fiddling with the optics and brushing dust off the bottles.

"Would that happen to be your friend from last night?"

"Yep."

He picked up his paper and leant against the opposite counter. They were silent for a couple of minutes before he peered over his paper.

"Is it love, then?"

She looked up and stared at him, downing her drink as she did so. She belched and shook the glass at him.

"Refill, please."

He took it from her and pulled on the pump. He placed the glass in front of her again and she swept it up, taking a large gulp of her drink.

"How often does he come in?" She asked.

"Most days. Would call him a sad bastard, but he keeps me belly full and all that."

"What time, mate?"

"About now, usually. You're going to give him a big smooch, then?"

She pushed the glass to one side and leant on the bar top.

"I'm going to snap his sodding neck."

Darren chuckled and returned to his paper. She drank the rest of her pint in silence. He peered over the top of the day's issue a couple of times, hoping to suss something out about her. She nudged the glass towards him.

"Don't stare, I'll turn you to stone. Whiskey, please."

"Darling, please don't embarrass yourself..."

"To who? Pour it."

He turned to the suspended bottle and clicked a measure into the squat glass. He placed it next to her and took her pint glass away. She threw the whiskey back.

"Going to the loo, give me a refill. If Butterwick comes in, keep him here."

She turned the corner to the ladies' room and saw the mop and bucket propped up against the door. She kicked them out of the way and stumbled into the cubicle. She sat there for a while, her head resting against the wall. Her brain felt like something was shoving it forward, as though she were nodding without moving her head. She could hear Darren start talking through the door, followed by an unnatural silence, even for a deserted pub. She left the cubicle and walked into the bar. Darren was gone.

"Hello again."

She looked into the snug and saw the same man as yesterday, in a similar suit, sat at a table. His back was straight, and the stool did not compliment his height. He looked like an over-eager school child.

"Ee-arr, have you seen where Darren's gone?"

"No."

His feline gaze met hers and he placed his hands flat on the table. She looked behind the bar. The cellar trapdoor was closed, and Darren's paper was folded like fresh linen on the other side of the bar. She turned to the man, who still stared at her. She approached his table and stood opposite him. They stayed like this, staring at one another, for what seemed like an age.

"Aren't you going to invite me to sit?" She said.

He shook his head once. His face had an unnerving calm, as if he was in a constant dream state. Everything about him carried the scent of artifice. Sheila pulled a stool out using her foot.

"The man you say you wish to meet. He is not coming."

Sheila cocked her head.

"Really? That right?"

He interwove his fingers and propped himself up by his forearms.

"The man you say you want to meet may well come in. But that is not the man you wish to meet, is it?"

She sat still and said nothing. He reached down to his left and produced a battered book. The same battered book she had flicked through earlier that week.

"You wish to know what we know. To feel what we feel. That is why you are here, is it not?"

His face looked gilded in the glow of the growing coal fire, the sweat on his cheeks blending together and taking on the hue of the flames.

"Yes."

He stood up and gave her the same penetrating look. He walked past her and out of the pub. She followed.

He stepped outside and took her around the corner. Wellington Road had no people walking down it, but every light in every front room burned bright. He did not try to link her arm or speak to her. They arrived at a buffed-out Standard Vanguard which sat next to the curb. There was a man inside it. He wore white and sat in the driver's seat, staring forwards. He did not move, but there was no stress around his face or his demeanour, as if it were the most natural thing in the world to sit still and stare straight ahead. They both got into the rear seat of the car. He placed the book in the front passenger seat. The driver started the ignition and they drove towards Wilbraham road.

"Where are we going, sir?"

"To meet the rest of our order."

Sheila nudged him with her elbow.

"Oh aye? Are you King Arthur, then? Or Lancelot?" She gritted her back teeth, wondering why she was in this car to begin with. He did not respond to her touch, but he did reply to her.

"I am only the Keeper. The Order is the greater will of Åkeran. It is the Light."

Sheila felt her throat twist with sickness. He tried her door handle, using two of her fingers, and found it too stiff to open. He saw her and put a soft hand on her shoulder. He raised his other hand and the car, which was not travelling fast, pulled over.

"I will not keep here if you do not want to be here."

She looked into the street. Aside from the car they were in and a bus which was crossing, there was no one around. If she left and they changed their minds, there would be no one to help. She pulled her fingers back out from underneath the latch and rested her hands on her legs again. He raised his hand and the driver started up again.

Orange lamp posts popped against the grey-blue twilight sky like meteors. The driver was sensible to the point of suspicious. The car never went at a speed which made the passengers lurch and took corners slowly. Manchester's city lights crested the rooftops as the car made its way up Birchfields Road. Sheila felt the man's lips moving at a pace next to her, but she could not pick out any words. He drove past the market stalls, where the vendors took their canopies apart and were busy putting their stock away. Pubs came to life yet had few people in them. The sky stopped being blue in the space of ten minutes and, as they made the final turn of their journey, the sky was black. They were in Grandview again, in another one of the dying neighbourhoods. Their car came to a halt.

"Come," he said, "Please."

He opened his door and held it open as she crawled out. The driver stayed put. They crossed the narrow road together. Only one house had its lights on, twenty yards away, and they went to this house. It was on the corner of a small crossroads and had a garden larger than the rest of the street, but only by a few square feet. They stood outside. Sheila could see one or two silhouettes in the front room, but no movement. There was no sound coming from the house.

The door opened. A man, a white man with red hair and moustache, stood in the doorway. His face voided all colour and he walked to them, his steps faltering as he arrived at the front gate. He got on one knee in reverence.

"Keeper. I am honoured." The man's voice did not suit his statement. The Keeper opened the gate and put his hand on the man's shoulder.

"Are you ready to welcome the light?"

"Yes, Keeper." The man removed his shirt. He had an enormous tattoo, jagged and warped from his own hand, of Åkeran's symbol. As primitive as it appeared, it was clear he had put effort and care into detailing it. His body was a canvas for whatever she was to witness.

"Be with us."

The man stood up and looked about the street in awe. Sheila followed his gaze. From alleys, ginnels, behind cars and from nearby streets, people were appearing. They wore white and had their heads up. Some wore blindfolds, others shaded glasses, some had their eyes closed as they walked. Many had their palms outstretched like devotional paintings. They gathered, one by one, at the house and stood in these same poses. She looked into the crowd and saw people of different colours. She leant over to the Keeper and whispered.

"Why are there immigrants here?"

He did not respond to her. She looked in the opposite direction and saw the broken man. People from Lillian's neighbourhood followed him like a prophet. His mouth was open a little, showing the wreckage of his jaw and teeth. Soon, the stretch of street in front of the house was packed with people who stood in silence. The Keeper took the man in his arms and released him.

"The order is ready for you," the Keeper said, "Who do you want to receive?" The man looked over at the broken man. He reached out an arm and they bore him forward. The Keeper got on one knee and kissed the broken man's hand, which she noticed had its ring and little fingers missing. He got to his feet and whispered something to the broken man, who nodded and waddled past him, into the house and into the front room. Sheila saw there was a small gap in the curtains. The broken man sat down on the floor, it looked like, and another shape moved to accommodate him. Sheila saw a flash of blonde hair on a small head and her heart started to thump.

"There are children in there..." she started to say. The words hung like a swarm of bees above them. The man looked at her and then at the Keeper, who kissed the man's forehead.

"Become. Drive away the darkness," he said, "So that we and our children may know only light." The man nodded and turned back into the house. He picked up a bottle, filled with pink fluid, and doused the door before closing it.

"There are children in there!" Sheila caught a wretch in her throat and went to vault the small fence.

She was halfway over when a hand grasped her from behind and she kicked back, hitting someone's ribs. Before she knew it, there were hands all over her, dragging her back. She tried to scream, and someone pushed some fabric into her mouth. They pulled her upright and held her in place. The Keeper still stood at the gate. A final silhouette made a circle around the front room and sat down.

At once, lurid fire sprang up across the downstairs and smoke regurgitated out of the house. The Keeper spread his arms and looked to the sky. Those holding Sheila dropped her to the ground joined him in his reverential pose. Sheila crawled towards the house, but the heat was already unbearable. She stared as the flames smashed their way out of the front windows and leapt up a floor. She heard a low moan, the spectre of a scream, through the flames, which died away in the fire's full-throated roar.

"Away from Darkness!" the Keeper cried out.

"It is the Light! It is the Light! It is the Light!" the crowd chanted. As soon as it was said, they began to disperse. Sheila stayed on the pavement for a moment and watched the house burn. Gaps emerged through the roof tiles as the blaze pushed into the attic. She leapt to her feet and ran after the Keeper, who was a few yards away. She jumped and hit him on the side of the head, which made him stumble off the kerb. He fell onto the cobbles and she pounced on him, throwing a punch at the back of his head. She turned him over and went to strike him again, only to be dragged off by other members of the order. They did not hit her but held her tight as she struggled against them. The Keeper got to his feet and waved the people to let go of her. They stood her up and let go of her but stayed next to her.

"We are all caught in the light of Åkeran," he remarked, "And Åkeran has no life, nor death." He walked back to his car, got in and it started away. The crowd dissipated back into the streets as quickly as they had arrived. Sheila walked, stunned, back to Birchfields Road as a fire engine, bells clattering, raced past her. He fell against a lamppost and slumped down to the floor. She stayed there until she became aware of the blue light washing over her. She turned around and saw a pair of men from Traffic.

"You're alright, love. We've got you."

She stood up and nodded at them.

"I'm alright lads. I've just come from round there. It's a bit much."

"Well, we're here now, we'll do our best with it."

"Aye, you lost usually do. Just one thing before you go, lads?"

She found herself in front of Fletcher's house. The lights burned in the house, and she could see the blousy woman from that morning traipse up and down the stairs. She went to the front door and knocked. The woman's shape appeared at the window and she pulled it open.

"Madam..."

"Get off my lawn, you deviant."

"Madam, please, I just need to see how she is."

"She'll survive. I should have you locked up, filth."

"Just, please, Madam..."

Sheila wedged her arm past the woman and shoulder-barged her away from the door. She ran up the stairs, with the woman close behind. She flung the bedroom door open and saw Fletcher lying there. A large bandage covered her nose and her lips were huge and purple.

"Sheila?"

"Fletch, I've just been to a burning, they're a mad bunch of bastards, they're very real and they're everywhere..."

Sheila felt five angry fingers entwine with her bun. The air vanished from her throat and her body tensed. The fingers yanked her head back and she flailed as they dragged her away from the door and across the landing, down the stairs and towards the front door. She caught her fingers in the gap between the hinges and the door. She looked up as the grip slackened and saw Fletcher's mum seize the front door. Sheila withdrew her fingers just as the door slammed in her face. The letter box opened.

"Don't you *dare* show your face at my house again, you slut!"

The letterbox closing had more finality in its harsh snap than the slamming door. She picked herself up and walked to the other side of the road. She walked up the road and saw a tearoom. There were three customers in there. One was a pro, scanning the street for business and police. The other two were a man in a tuxedo, red rose in lapel, who was playing with the hair of an effeminate young man with dirty blonde curls. All of them looked at Sheila in her dirty tunic and averted their gazes. She put a penny on the counter.

"Tea, please. Strong."

The proprietor pushed the penny back to her. He disappeared for a second and returned with a full cup.

"My compliments, officer."

She took it. They smiled at each other through mutual tired eyes. She sat in the corner nearest the back. The pro stood up and looked at Sheila, unsure of whether to put up defences or ask for help. Sheila removed her cap and put it down on the seat next to her. The pro smiled and walked into the night.

Sixteen

The rain came down in steady patter. A dormant yet malignant
headache announced itself as she walked over to her house,
and she gritted her teeth. She kicked the front gate aside. It
ricocheted off the wall with a bang and caught the back of her
ankle as she stepped into the garden.

"Just fuck off!" She spat, turning and booting it with her
other foot. A shard of wood flew off the corner where she
struck it and it closed, as if it had learned its lesson. Rodney
was not prowling or curled up in the garden today. A huge
cloud towered in the distance like a great iron weight about to
fall on the city. She saw no one in the window, but all the lights
in the house were on. The letterbox snipped at her fingers as
she went for the key and she pulled back, sucking on the small
cut made in her fingers.

"Oh, bugger it all!" she yelled, rearing back and about to land a kick on the door handle. The door creaked open a little, and Rodney darted through the gap, vaulted the face and bolted into the street. Sheila stayed herself and nudged the door open. There was no one there, and a small breeze ran through the house, making her shiver.

"Alice?" She stepped into the house. The stillness, on the street and inside, was overwhelming, as if the whole neighbourhood was holding its breath. She looked behind the door and saw the ancient rounders bat that Alice kept there. She took it and started stalking through the house. The rear door in the kitchen swayed a little in the breeze. She went over, keeping her back to the cabinets, and looked through the back. The outhouse was wide open and empty. She closed the door and went into the front room. Music warbled from the wireless, set below Alice's usual destructive volume. A cup of tea, flanked by a pile of biscuits, lay between the two armchairs. Sheila turned and looked under the stairs. Alice's coats and bags were hung up, as was her apron.

A loose floorboard yawned from above and Sheila slipped off her shoes, one by one, and began to place her toes like a dancer, the bat in one hand as she made her way up the stairs. The landing loomed into view and only her bedroom door was open. She put her hand on the doorknob and counted down from three in her head. She threw it open and rushed in.

The green netting above the window shimmered in the gentle wind. There was nothing different about the room. She turned about and made her way past her room, as chaotic as ever, but no one hiding in it. Alice's room was at the front. She again counted down from three and burst the door open. Alice's bedsheets were pressed flat and the cushions laid out in a neat row of three across her pillows. Sheila took a step back and got down on her knees to look under the bed. She could see right through to the other side, only a pair of shoes and a pair of slippers sat in the way. Her cupboards were wide open, ordered and neat. She leant against the wall and placed the rounders bat against the door frame.

She took a couple of steps across the landing and went into her room. She wrenched her uniform off, balling the tunic and skirts up and throwing them across her room. She took a breath and picked up a simple grey jumper and brown skirt. She put them on. Each felt like a ton of weight, the commingled shame and relief of being kicked out of the force pulling on her frame. She sat on the bed and put her head in her hands. The finality in the silence around her put an end to any thought or anything else in her mind. She felt as if, whatever purpose she had served, she was finished.

"Love?"

Sheila jumped and saw Alice stood at the door, wearing what looked like an old nightie.

"Bloody nora, Al. Where've you been? Thought someone'd done you in when I got home."

"You didn't come home last night. Everything alright?"

Sheila wiped her eye reflexively.

"They've binned me off. Took them long enough, but I'm no longer a copper."

"Oh, Sheila..."

She started to cry. Alice came over and rocked Sheila's head against her stomach. Sheila had a minute and then composed herself.

"I don't know what I'm going to do now. You're everything I've got left and I don't want to spend my life working in the bloody mills for pittance. What am I going to do?"

Alice cocked her head.

"Sheila, what happened last night?"

"Got drunk, said some things I shouldn't have to someone I thought was a mate. Got called in the office and that was that."

"You had me worried, you know."

Sheila pulled away from Alice's embrace.

"Look, love, you're very caring and I love that you love me so much, but you're not my mum, I don't need to ring you up or leave you a note when I want to have a drink or two."

"No, that's not what I mean. I mean, a friend of yours came looking for you last night, said that you might have been in trouble and did I know where you were."

"You what?"

"A big bloke. Looked like he were wearing his Sunday best."

"Was he wearing white?"

"Aye, he were. Well, he is."

Sheila stood up and felt her legs contract into a half crouch and her fists clench, ready to run.

"What are you talking about?"

"Well, he knocked on today and asked for you today, said you'd be back in a bit so I let him in. Is he not downstairs?"

The front door slammed. Sheila looked out the window to her right and saw groups of people, wearing white, emerge from the rear houses and the back alley. The back gate opened, and they shuffled in, all with their eyes closed. Sheila pushed Alice out of the way and turned onto the stairs.

He stood at the bottom, looking at her with eyes that seemed painted open. He started taking steps up to her.

"Åkeran is the light and Åkeran is the way."

He took his time. Sheila closed herself in the bathroom, stood on the toilet seat and took the lid off the cistern. She jumped down and raised it to her shoulder height, waiting for the Keeper or his followers to try and break her door down.

"Come on, you bunch of cunts! I'll fill the fucking lot of you in, fucking come on then!"

His steps went past the door and she heard him mumble something to Alice, and then steps going towards the front bedroom. She could hear Alice's vibrato through the walls as he spoke to her.

"No, don't you bloody dare lay a finger on her, you big oily twat, I'll rip your cock off, you bad bastard, you!"

The door closed down the hall. Slow, heavy steps came across the landing, as did the sound of liquid hitting the carpet. Droplets emerged under the door and the steps carried on down the stairs.

Paraffin.

"Oh my god! Shit!"

Sheila dropped the cistern lid, which broke into pieces. She tore open the bathroom door and saw him stood at the foot of the stairs.

"Away from Darkness!" he cried out, scratching a match into life.

"*It is the Light! It is the Light! It is the Light!*" the crowd outside chanted. He dropped the match.

The flames moved like an earthquake fissure, snaking up the staircase and engulfing the door next to her. She tried to close it, but already the fire was too intense. The fibres and threads on her sweater ignited and crawled across her shoulders. She started to panic and slapped herself to try and stem the flames, but she could already feel her neck and the back of her hair start to scorch. As she wheeled and swung her arms, she caught the door with her heel and it closed, but the embryonic flames already glimmered on her side of the door.

She opened the toilet lid and plunged her head into it, before rearing back and feeling the water slosh out the flames on her back, stinging a little on her spine. She swatted out the rest of the flames on her shoulders and then fell to the ground, writhing and coughing as smoke filled the room like a locust swarm. Her eyes no longer opened as the heat carried on, relentless and greedy, consuming the door and scrambling up the ceiling. She pushed the small window open. There was nothing to break her fall and she was not sure that she could fit through it in the first place. The smoke shot out of it and overwhelmed the tiny passage. The floor began to sear her feet. She reached out, hacking through the smothering smoke, and her fingers found the window. She reached through with both of her hands and pulled her bodyweight by the brickwork. She got as far as her waist before she stopped. Below her, smoke leaked through the kitchen window. She looked up at the houses opposite and began to scream for help. There were faces in the windows, cat's eyes in darkness, which looked on, impassive, at the spectacle in front of them. She could smell gas. She looked down.

The explosion made short work of the brickwork encasing her. In that moment, soaring and tumbling through the air like a wounded hawk, the images of the neighbourhood, the sky, the world, flashed by, hundreds of times per second, a giant film reel played at enormous speed. They dissolved into one another, a warped bowl of unmixed paint running together. As the world darkened, as the ground approached, as the end neared, she discerned a face, framed in the golden haze of the fire, smiling at her and getting larger.

A set of cobbles, like huge, rotten teeth, took over her vision and her face slammed against them.

A bunch of plodding feet woke her. The low grunting of a fire engine was somewhere nearby. The smell of water against stone and asphalt coupled itself with the close mist, from rain water and fire hoses alike, a great, empathetic hand. She twitched a finger and a mortifying heat ran like a giant blade across her shoulders and down her back. She cried out. Voices nearby became agitated. She tried to pull herself upright and found she could not gain a grip with her right hand. She brought it in front of her face and started to hyperventilate.

Her fingers, from the index to her little finger, were missing, as was a section of her palm. The flames had cauterized it in the blast. Scar tissue and burns stretched across her hand like moss on an antiquated sculpture, left to ruin by time and weather. It was now that she felt the pain. She cried out and began to shriek, her throat scratching and cracking with every drawn-out, hooting breath. A group of people surrounded her as the shock overpowered her. Something pierced her back and a wave of non-feeling washed over her, as though erasing her whole being.

"Wait, wait, get Wolfe, she's waking up."

The crisp hospital air settled up her nose and on her dry tongue. Someone was stood at the end of the bed. She did not recognise the voice. She made to lift a hand to scratch at her eye. The stiffness in her arm stopped her after an inch of movement. She closed her eyes and knew she could do nothing about the pain. It would listen to no reason or bargain and she was trapped. Someone entered the room. The three dark figures stood at the foot of her bed, all shrouded in darkness save for their eyes, which glowed in the light of the corridor to the left.

"Sheila? It's Wolfe. Can you hear me?"

Sheila nodded.

"Sheila, we can see you've had a hard time of it. We need to ask you some questions."

She opened her left eye. She could not see through or feel her right one.

"Can we just…" She ran and flicked her tongue around the front of her mouth. Her four front teeth were gone.

"Sheila, this is vital. Did you set that fire yourself?"

"No, Wolfe, I didn't."

"Alright."

"Where's Alice?"

Sheila saw him move to her right, but she could not move to meet his eyes. She heard him plant his hand on the bed near her arm.

"I'm sorry, Sheel." He touched her forearm and she flinched.

"Why are they bothering with me, sir? I'm a bag of bones. No use."

"Don't say that, Sheila. You're going to be fine, you're alright."

Sheila laughed.

"I'm knackered, boss. I'm worn out. Done. Just tell the nurse to get in here with a big bastard syringe of something and all'll be right. Speaking of which, where am I?"

"Wythy, love. Get rested up, now, Sheel. We'll be back in the morning."

He and the other officers left. The murky ward was silent, save for the deep breathing of sleeping patients around her. She lifted her left arm and saw her hand, bearing a huge stitched scar which snaked down her forearm like a mountain train line. Her fingers would not bend as far as they used to. She touched her face and felt a coarse web of bandages on her head. She heard footsteps come over and a familiar voice.

"Evening, constable."

The nurse came round to where Sheila could see her.

"Blood and sand, nurse. I'm sorry we couldn't have met under better.."

The nurse looked at her, almost nose to nose. Her eyes had a faint disgust behind them, as well as a note of confused contrition.

"Listen, listen. You aren't meant to be here."

"Well, I'm in bits and this is a hospital, ain't it? Fuck you on about?"

The nurse seized her by the shoulder and covered her mouth as she cried out. Her eyes lit up with a determined rage and she clamped her hand down harder.

"You were ready to receive us. We can't leave you here. Åkeran is the light and the way."

Sheila felt a pocket of flesh on the nurse's palm slip into her open mouth and bit. Her canines caught the nurse, who loosened her grip and yelled out. Sheila jerked her left leg and caught the nurse in the back of the head with her knee, who fell forward onto the bed unconscious and slipped off, onto the floor. Sheila sat up and wiggled her feet. They hurt, but they were there. She was not sure if they would hold her up. She pushed herself off the bed and stood for a second before falling against the wall. Her legs were black from bruising and burns. She hopped forward and felt a needle scratch inside her left bicep which made her stomach turn, and a pair of bottles on a stand crashed to the floor behind her. She looked and saw the drips in her arm. She brought her right arm over, now bandaged over from where her remaining finger and thumb had been amputated. She pressed the stump of her hand against them and pushed. It felt as if she was pulling her veins out themselves. Still, she ground against them, and they started to yield. The blood feed popped out and dripped against the wall like hot wax. The saline drip emerged just after, shining like a fresh tooth. She took a breath, and became aware of a presence to her right.

A man in a hospital gown stood in the centre of the room. He stared at her and outstretched his arms. He started to walk towards her, limping as he went. She hopped again, trying to get away. He was almost at her bed. She saw his legs were bound by huge casts, which started to crack and flake away. Blood and skin came down with them as he walked, exposing charred fat and bone.

"We must accept and receive Åkeran as Åkeran receives us," he said, "It is the Light."

She arrived at the ward doors, which would not swing open. She pushed against them and ran her shoulder into them and she started to cry out.

"Has the whole bloody world gone mad! Help!"

She heard his steps behind her and she turned. He lunged at her and took her by her collar. In turn, she kicked at his shin, which knocked him back. She grabbed him and pulled back, as if she was to dive through the floor, bringing him with her. They smacked into the doors. The small lock burst through the other side of the door with a snap and the door opened slowly, as if it was hesitant to let them go. He pulled himself on top of her and put one hand around her neck, followed by the other. He pressed down on her voice box and she started to flail her arms. A look of calm instilled itself on his face and he renewed the pressure. Spots started to appear in Sheila's vision. Then she felt something cold and straight in her left hand. The drip stand. She jabbed the stand up to his head, not sure if it would hit him or if it would do anything.

She missed his head, but the stand hook caught him in his jugular. Blood wept forth from the cut and hit her in her only eye. He released his grip. He made to stand and slipped in his own blood, falling onto his back. There was a grim crunch as he fell. His tibia poked through the remnants of his cast and the two parts of his broken leg moved in different directions as he struggled on the floor. She spat out his blood and tried to pull herself along the floor.

The amount of gore made this near impossible for her, and her eye started to burn. Blinded, she carried on thrashing on the floor. It was no use. She was overcome with rage and fright, and started yelling. She felt urgent footsteps rumble along the floor towards her.

"Madam? Can you hear me? Are you injured, madam...good God..."

Two pairs of hands picked her up by her shoulders and her ankles and took her away. The pain and adrenaline swept through her. Her vision darkened to nothing.

Seventeen

She awoke under a low, grey ceiling. A sliver of light shimmered across the ceiling as if through water. Footsteps echoed like falling rocks somewhere in the distance. She kept still and focused on the scene above her with her only eye. Leather bit into her wrists and she could feel another strap cut across her ribs. She did not move her head, which rested on hard wood. Hours passed before she heard movement outside. A series of steely sounds smacked together, hinges squealing as her door opened and something slid on the floor before it banged closed again.

Bland as they were, she could recognise the cells in Anderson Street anywhere. She did not want to look around, or be bothered by anything or anyone. The routine carried on another three times, punctuating the seamless time spent watching the light, moving away from her and faded away.

The door closed and the person took several slow steps over to her. She closed her eyes, expecting to see the light darkened from under her eyelids from a pillow jammed over her face, or to feel something sharp at her throat.

"Blah blah light et cetera. Get on with it, you mad bastard."

"With what, Sheel?"

She opened her eyes and saw Gibbons. Her eyes were baggy and inflamed. If Gibbons had had one or two errant curls on any given shift, it was a topic of station gossip. She never looked anything but ready. Sheila reach her hand out instinctively, forgetting that she had lost it.

"Gibbo?"

Gibbons took her arm and knelt next to the bed.

"What in Christ's name happened to you, eh?"

"Stuck me nose where I shouldn't have."

Gibbons sat down and placed her hand around Sheila's bare left cheek.

"I only hold hands at first, Gibbo," Sheila laughed, "and its a bit dodge that you had to tie me up, and all. Not into all that-"

"Shut up, Sheila," Gibbons replied, tired and humourless, "I nearly had a sodding heart attack when they said you were on the critical list, never mind that you'd killed another bloody patient and knocked out a nurse."

"They wanted me dead, they were with that bunch of nutters who burnt down me house."

"Sheel, you're not accused of witchcraft, don't be ridiculous."

"Why else did they burn down my fucking house, eh?"

"Please don't swear at me, I'm not your sergeant any more, but do me that courtesy, at least."

Sheila cried out in a manner both of a laugh and a sob. She jerked her head a couple of inches to the left, which was as far as she could move, out of Gibbons' hand.

"Well, believe what you like, but they were going to kill me. I'm not saying any more."

"Sheila, please talk to me, you're acting like you're already dead…"

"Am I not, though? My life's been a complete shit-show ever since Marion left. You know it, I know it." Her voice became empty and breathy. "I don't know what I was thinking, staying in this job. Now I don't even have that. Don't even have a roof. Don't have both my hands, for fuck's sake. And they're going to chuck me in the bin with women who pimp out their kids and drown them before the neighbours find out."

Gibbons wiped at her eyes and sniffed. Sheila shook her head and didn't look at her.

"And that's where you're taking me, isn't it?" Gibbons leant across her. Sheila groaned as her body protested against the touch. With a soft *click*, the strap across her chest loosened and Gibbons pulled it out from the buckle. She carried on, slowly, to each strap at Sheila's hands and feet.

"Quiet now, Sheel. Come on, up you get."

Gibbons pulled her up right and guided her off the bed. Something clinked on the floor under Sheila's foot. She looked down and saw braces on both of her bandaged legs. She started to fall forwards and Gibbons' caught her with a hand to the breast bone, pushing her back upright.

"Easy does it, come on."

The pair walked alongside one another, Sheila keeping to Gibbons' steps like her shadow. Her braces scraped a little against the floor as she edged forward. They turned into the cell corridor. There was no one else in sight and all the cell doors were open. Above the steps, the desk sergeant was gone. Each step up was an ordeal and Gibbons took to lifting Sheila as they went. She propped Sheila against the desk like a stuffed animal as she took a breather and mopped her brow. Sheila looked around for other officers, but the lobby was deserted. At that time of night, under those lights and with no one around, Anderson Street looked like the lobby of a grand but neglected hotel.

"Right, let's go." Gibbons pulled Sheila up again and they made their way to the front door. The rain slashed across the street in the bullying wind. The Mini cooper, still looking as if it might fall to pieces at any moment, sat just off the pavement. Sheila's bandages took on water and began to weigh her down as they went down the steps. Gibbons cap blew off her head and started rolling and dancing down the road as if it were mocking her. She looked over at it, and then carried on going without a word. Sheila collapsed against the side of the car, grunting as she pushed herself off by her forearms. Gibbons opened the back door and ushered Sheila into the back seat, her heavy breath against Sheila's cheek providing the only heat in the storm. Sheila lay down and tried to curl up as Gibbons popped the boot open and pulled out a blanket, chucking it onto her before coming round and wrapping her up, pulling the blanket taut over Sheila's legs. Gibbons got into the driver's seat. She pulled out a box from under her seat.

"These are yours, I believe?" She said, shaking the biscuits at Sheila.

"Don't take the piss, Gibbo."

"Just trying to be civil, Sheel."

"Bugger your civil."

Gibbons started the car.

"Sheel, you might want to sit up. Please. I don't want to kill you on the journey."

Sheila pushed herself upright with her left arm and pulled herself level with the window. She looked at the street as it disappeared from view. From Oxford Road, past Spinningfields and Blackfriars, She knew where they were going. So many times she had sat in the back of a van, listening to the pleading and wailing from a prisoner as they made their way there, felt the impact of an inmate's knee or foot or head against the metal partition. People went into Springfield all the time, but few got out. It was the perfect hiding place for people who were surplus to requirements, or had crossed the wrong people, or the wrong organisations, and she knew she would likely die there. She traced idle patterns on the window with her finger, focusing on the point of wetness on her finger and the benign drumming of rain on the roof, lulling her senses as much as she could. Cheetham Hill loomed into view as Gibbons turned onto Middleton Road. She had not put the sirens on, which was unusual. She liked to rush to places, having time nor patience for traffic. It did not seem to matter this night, as the road were empty. Sheila saw the turning for Crumpsall Lane and felt nothing. All sensation felt as if it had vanished, save for her heart beating like a sparrow's wings.

Gibbons carried on going. The packed streets soon gave way and distant lights trembled on the sides of the Pennines. It did not look like a short cut, or resemble a scenic route. Soon they were in Middleton, around streets which Sheila did not know the names of, but remembered how they looked. Sheila looked at Gibbons, whose gaze didn't move from the road ahead.

"Don't prolong me misery, just drop me at the bin."

"We're not going to the bin. You're certainly not going to the bin, I won't entertain it."

Sheila sat up.

"You what?"

"I told you I was fond of you, Sheel. We both know what happens to women who go there. Just relax and let me take you somewhere else."

Sheila leant forward into the gap between the seats.

"Sarge, are you sure? They'll skin you alive if they find out."

"They won't. Sit back before I turn the car around."

Sheila rested her head on the side of the passenger seat. The car slowed at a red light. The box rattled again near her head.

"Can we be civil now?" Gibbo said, holding the box out with her familiar, parental look. Sheila took the box and smiled. She opened it and ate one, nibbling rather than stuffing it into her face. Her molars ached as she chewed.

"Sorry I was such a bad bobby, Sarge," she said, mouth half full.

"Give over, Sheel. Plenty of B Division hang around the London Road arches, many more are bent in other ways. You're nothing like them." Gibbons set off again and the street lights became less frequent. "You might not have been smacking people with truncheons or arresting Mr. Big, but you cared. And you were a pain in the arse, granted, *and you eat with your mouth full,* but you weren't mean and horrible."

The only light now was coming from Gibbons' headlights. The rain still drummed against the roof as trees and the edges of fields were in view just beside the car. A huge pair of hills sat in front of them like guards at a gate.

"You know before, Gibbo, when you said I shouldn't act like I'm already dead?"

"Yes?"

"Don't talk like I am, either. I'm going to get some shut eye now. Wake me up in a bit?"

"Of course, Sheila."

Sheila put her head against the window. The road became rockier and her head started to vibrate on the window as the car did. She felt her heart dip and dive as the adrenaline ebbed against her veins and stopped flowing. She pulled the blanket higher to her chin. Sheila started to drift. The rocking in the car became more and more pronounced and her head began to bounce a little off the door.

"Gibbo, are you driving us across the moon here?"

"Hush, Sheel. You have a sleep."

"Yeah, right, I will."

She put her head down again as the car stopped shaking and the road felt smoother. The seat thumped against her back.

"God's teeth, Gibbo, this old thing's coming apart. Are these seats broke?"

Gibbons did not reply.

"Hello, Sarge?"

"*Sheel?*"

The voice was strangled hoarse. Sheila felt her heart quicken again and she sat up.

"Sarge, did you hear that?"

"Hear what?"

"*Sheila!*" the cry came from the boot. Sheila did not need Gibbons to tell her. She knew the accent anywhere. It was Fletcher. Gibbons started to speed up. The pummelling on Sheila's back intensified, knocking her forward with every hit, each strike making her panic more and more.

"Gibbo, what's happening?"

Gibbons said nothing as the engine whined under the pressure of the hill and accelerator. Sheila wedged her forearm against the back of her seat and set her teeth. She pulled and pulled, feeling the seat frame dig into her tender, wounded arm. She pulled until the leather started to tear off the padding. Her bandage came away, caught by the frame, which in turn caught her stitches and pulled them out of her arm, dragging her skin away to reveal more and more of her arm like an evening glove. Sheila's tight grunt broke under the weight of her effort and she started to yell, getting higher and higher in pitch as the frame dug deeper and deeper into her, forcing the seat forward by a small, near imperceptible amount as it seemed to fight back against her.

The seat clunked forward and, with her other hand, she pulled the seat forward. Fletcher's eyes flashed for a moment as Sheila tried to force the seat down further. Gibbons tapped the brakes, which made Sheila lurch back and roll into the foot well, letting go of the seat which snapped back up like a bear trap. She tried to kick her legs and felt something pinioning them together, which made her braces squeeze against her injured legs. She cried out.

"What in fuck's name are you doing, Gibbo?"

"I told you to be quiet, Sheel. You should have listened. It is the Light."

Gibbons turned her body to face Sheila. She raised her baton and brought it down onto Sheila's head.

Eighteen

The handbrake clicked four times into its highest position and Gibbons got out, bouncing the driver's door off the side of the mini. Sheila snapped awake, her two-figure blurred vision coming into one consonant view like sliding doors as Gibbons opened her side of the car and dragged her out by her shoulders. Sheila took hold of the back of the passenger seat in desperation, only for Gibbons' baton to smash into her fingers, releasing her grip. She hit her head against the chassis and then the cake-like mud next to the wheel. Gibbons left her there, rolling in agony, as she opened the boot.

There was not one, but two sets of choked screams. One was lower in pitch than Fletcher's. Sheila pushed herself onto her left side to see. There, like sacrificial animals, lay Fletcher and Meredith. Their eyes were dazzling, their naked fear exacerbated by the crimson brake light. Each of them had their eyes on Sheila, as if her shattered body could knit itself back together and free them all. Then she became aware that her head bandage had come loose. A gust of Pennine wind wafted over her face and she felt the cold burn against her exposed flesh. She yelped out and rocked onto her back.

Gibbons appeared and pulled her by her feet up the rest of the hill. Below her, the county lights stretched on like starry reflections on water. Manchester burned brightest, becoming scattered and scarce the further out the lights became, as though someone had dropped thousands of precious stones across a dark floor. The earth beneath her became harder and wetter, soaking through her dressings before balling them up and tearing them off her. Ice scraped against her back like glass paper.

"Put me down, you old bitch!"

Gibbons carried on dragging her. The ground levelled out and Gibbons slowed down. They stopped. Sheila heard Gibbons' strained breathing, as well as the breathing of others. Sheila began to rant.

"Bloody Gibbo! It was you, wasn't it? What did that girl ever do to you? She lost everyone and everything and you strung her up and blamed me, you did! You're as bad as them, you know. Dicky Bogarde, my arse, you're a bloody disgrace, you are! I hope you die slow, you horrible cunt! Get off my friends, what have they ever done to you?"

A group of hands took her around her limbs and lifted her up. In the darkness, she discerned figures in white. They stood at regular intervals up the hill. The wind billowed in their robes, but none of them moved. Gibbons reappeared, dragging Fletcher by the ankles into the gloom, howling into a gag as she went. A pair of people from the Order pulled Meredith in the same direction. His body was limp, and blood was smeared over his face like a tribal mask. Gibbons appeared out of the darkness.

"Sheila, listen to me..." she began.

"Get fucked, Gibbo! Fuck off back to your shanty, *you fucking parasite!*" Sheila barked. She could taste blood in her throat. Gibbons stood still and composed, and took off her grey coat and tunic. She removed her cap and dropped it on the floor.

"Sheila. Åkeran is the light and the way. We can't go back to the way we were. This town has been through too much. It needs to move to a new age. Åkeran helps us to find our new strength. Don't you see?" She rose and Sheila lolled her head.

"Sheila, will you be with us?"

Sheila said something that she couldn't make out. She gestured at the people holding Sheila, who brought her forward. She leant in. Sheila pressed her cheek, still gawping with open wound, against Gibbons'.

"Are you ready to welcome the light, Sheila?"

She paused. Sheila whispered.

"Murderer."

She snapped her jaw forward and Gibbons yelped in pain. She recoiled, spinning and stumbling as she went, and held her ear, now silken with bright blood. As they pulled her away, Sheila spat out Gibbons' earlobe.

"Get on with it, then, you bunch of..."

An unseen hand forced a gag into her mouth and pulled it taut behind her head. Sheila could not kick her legs but she struggled as much as she could. Someone in white saw to Gibbons in the dark. She stopped yelling and walked away. The figure stepped into her view. The Keeper had the same suit on as the last time. He wiped his hands with a silk handkerchief as he walked towards her. He stood in front of her and gestured at the people who held her. They removed her gag.

"Be with us. Please."

"Fuck off."

He stepped back.

"As you wish." He walked into the dark and they replaced her gag. The distant figures emerged out of the dark and stood closer around them all. The wind picked up, as if nature itself took to its feet. There was a sloshing sound. Fletcher's muted voice became hysterical and cut through it all. The empty jerry can banged across the ground. Something came to light.

A torch. It illuminated an obscene still life – The Keeper held up the flame, as Gibbons kneeled, her arms outstretched like a nesting bird, a bloody noontime shadow across her white blouse, with Fletcher and Meredith, bound, weeping and hopeless, propped by their backs against their knees.

Sheila closed her eye. A pair of sharp nails dug into the eyelids and pulled them apart as another hand seized her chin and held her head still. Her breathing deepened and got faster. The Keeper looked to his left. She followed his gaze. She caught her breath. She thought he was dead.

The broken man nodded.

"Away from Darkness!" came a shout.

"It is the Light! It is the Light! It is the Light!" the crowd chanted. Sheila cried out as the torch dropped.

The ground exploded into an unholy mass of flames and swallowed the scene. Fletcher and Meredith disappeared on the instant, as did the Keeper, but Gibbons kept her shape, her outstretched silhouette visible for a few seconds before they disappeared like closed eyes in the fire.

The Broken Man walked into the fire. But it did not take him. He stood in the midst of it as his clothes burned off. His body bore ancient scars like seems in homespun clothing. He removed his glasses and reached into the air. He reached into the air and emitted a loud noise. It did not sound like a man in pain, or much like a man at all. The ground shook.

His body grew in size and began to wrap around up itself like a cirrus cloud. Soon he bore no human shape at all, but a wretched other. The shape continued to grow and feed into itself, before resting above the fire and pulsing in a perfect symmetry. The clouds split. Sheila looked up. A slit of light, like a distant supernova, split apart from the menagerie of stars and overtook the night around it. It then expanded out and bathed the light in oppressive light. The fingers did not let go of Sheila's eye. She started to cry out in pain. Her eyeball itself felt as if it was singed, and her lashes wilted under the intense heat the apparition gave off.

"It is the Light! It is the Light! It is the Light!"

The fingers let go of her eye, and the people holding her up let go of her. She hit the ground and put a hand to her face, floundering in her blindness. There was nothing left for her to do, so she pressed herself up from the floor. She hauled herself along by her one working leg, her vision now an impenetrable black. Even if she was to get lost in peat bog or fall off a cliff, it would offer a better relief to her suffering than what the order would give. She started to yell out into the darkness with each step. She could no longer form words. Each noise blurred into the other as she went, limping, manic, raving, into the night.

**

22nd October 1960

Dear Sheila,

I'm sorry I've not got round to replying to you. I had no idea you had sent any letters until after everything was in the paper. Either you've got a crap memory or I'm a crap lover. I could have done with one of your letters. Lancs constab was a lonely place for girls like us and I could have used one of your steamy ones.

I did traffic duty up in Rawtenstall. No joke. So stuff you and your 'you can't drive for toffee' attitude. Not that it matters who drives. They'd let the police dogs have a go up there, bugger all for them to do. I'm not with the force anymore. It bored me to tears. The men drank all the time because they could. I would have done too, but everyone spies on everyone there, you know.

My mum died last year. I'm in her house now, back in the city. Landlord's a complete tit but he leaves well alone. I can't wait to have you back and wrap us both up in my bed again. Who needs hot water bottles, anyway? I miss you stroking my hair every day. No one treated me like that ever. I miss you calling me 'my love.' I miss you pretending to be hard all the time because it got me going. I miss you taking the piss out of my make-up.

Your old lot weren't any use. Told me you were lost on the moors, but you're too careful for that. Cars get lost on the moors, sheep get lost up there, but not you. You, my gorgeous, my tough nut. You're out there still. But I know that you're scared. I know that you're cold and desperate and hungry and need help. I know that you want me to get you. So I'm going to bring you home.

I love you and I miss you so much, darling.

Don't worry, I'm on my way. I'm coming to find you.

All my love,

Marion.

Printed in Great Britain
by Amazon